"I just can't do it!"

Mr. Talbot gave each set of partners in our science class a frog. He explained how to pin the frog down so that we could see its stomach. "I'll do it," Mark volunteered, trying to help me get through it.

Mr. Talbot went on to talk about where to make the incisions, what to look for inside the frog, and how it did or didn't relate to the human body. My head started spinning, and my stomach felt out of control, too. I knew I wouldn't be able to listen much longer without getting sick!

Finally I jumped out of my chair. "I just can't do it!" I cried. I couldn't believe it. Before, I had been afraid of making a scene, and there I was, openly defying a teacher — our brand-new teacher.

Look for these and other books
in the Sleepover Friends Series:

Lauren Saves the Day

Susan Saunders

AN
APPLE
PAPERBACK

SCHOLASTIC INC.
New York Toronto London Auckland Sydney

ISBN 0-590-44355-0

Copyright © 1991 by Daniel Weiss Associates, Inc. All rights reserved. Published by Scholastic Inc. APPLE PAPERBACKS is a registered trademark of Scholastic Inc. SLEEPOVER FRIENDS is a registered trademark of Daniel Weiss Associates, Inc.

12 11 10 9 8 7 6 5 4 3 2   1 2 3 4 5 6/9

Printed in the U.S.A.   28

First Scholastic printing, June 1991

Lauren Saves the Day

Chapter 1

"Hey, slow down," Henry Larkin called to Patti Jenkins as she raced down the hall. "I can hardly keep up!"

"He'd better not try or he'll pass out from exhaustion before we get to the science lab," Kate Beekman said to me.

I'm Lauren Hunter. We're all in 5B, Mrs. Mead's class, at Riverhurst Elementary. We were pretty excited since we were getting out of social studies to go see the new science room. Patti was way ahead because she was even more excited than the rest of us! Science is her favorite subject. She's even in an afterschool club called the Quarks, which is for super-smart science students.

Stephanie Green giggled. "You might as well

save your breath, Henry," she said. "Mad Scientist Jenkins probably can't even hear you." Along with Patti and Kate, Stephanie's my other best friend.

Patti whirled around from the front of the line. "Oh, sorry, you guys," she apologized. "I guess I got a little carried away."

"That's okay," I reassured her. "If there was something in that room that I liked as much as you like science, I'd walk fast, too."

"Something like Kevin DeSpain?" Stephanie asked me.

"Definitely!" I nodded. Kate rolled her eyes. Kevin DeSpain is one of the stars of *Made for Each Other* on TV, and he's really gorgeous. But Kate thinks he's a worse actor than Benji. She wants to be a director someday, so she's really into television and films. Still, she does admit that Kevin's nice — and handsome! We met him once when he was filming a movie in Riverhurst.

We turned the corner into the science room, and Patti, Stephanie, Kate, and I rushed to a table up front. Henry grabbed a seat at the table behind Patti. They've sort of been an item since Valentine's Day.

2

"Mark Freedman!" Pete Stone shouted, pointing to the skeleton hanging from a pole near the chalkboard. "It's your girlfriend!"

"Yeah, but that's better than you'll ever do!" Mark said, laughing.

The entire class cracked up — even Pete. They're always teasing each other.

The science room was really cool! There were all sorts of neat things set up around the room. "Look!" Larry Jackson said. "It's Patti Jenkins' brain!" Patti blushed. Larry was talking about a huge plastic model of a brain sitting on the counter near the windows. Once my mother had told me that a human brain is about the size of two fists together. This one was three times that size! I didn't know anyone whose head was that big!

Next to the brain were models of an eye and an ear. There was also a cabinet in the back of the room with lots of microscopes. They were really neat — just like the kind the mad scientists always use in "Friday Night Chillers"! "Friday Night Chillers" is a double-feature horror movie that's on every Friday night. Since Kate loves all kinds of movies, and since the four of us spend practically *every* Friday night together, we often end up watching them at our sleepovers. And since it was Friday afternoon, I knew I'd be watching one that night.

In the beginning, it was just Kate and me. We lived practically next door to each other — just one house away on Pine Street — so we played together a lot. (Now I live across town in a really old house on Brio Drive.) When we started kindergarten, we began sleeping at each other's houses on Friday nights. It got to be a regular thing. Kate's dad called us the Sleepover Twins.

Then, the summer before fourth grade, Stephanie moved to Riverhurst, and we were in the same class. I really liked her and thought Kate would, too, so I invited Stephanie to a sleepover. To say Kate and Stephanie didn't hit it off would be putting it mildly! But they kept trying to make it work for my sake — and eventually it did. So the Sleepover Twins became the Sleepover Trio.

When Patti showed up in Mrs. Mead's class at the end of the first week of school this year, Stephanie recognized her from their old school in the city. She asked us if Patti could join in on the sleepovers, too. Kate and I liked Patti so much that we agreed right away. We had to change our name again, but it was worth it. Now we're the Sleepover Friends!

Kate looked around the classrooom. "I wonder where our new teacher is?" she said. "What do you think she'll be like?"

"It would be okay with me if she were like Mrs. Mead — but with less homework," I said. Mrs. Mead is pretty nice, but she gives more assignments than any other fifth-grade teacher.

"No way," Henry protested. "I hope she's more like Ms. Gilberto." Henry is a big cutup, and Mrs. Mead sends him to the principal, Mrs. Wainwright, a lot! But Ms. Gilberto, our art teacher, is more of a pushover, and lets him get away with just about everything!

"I don't care what she's like, just as long as she's not like Mrs. Milton," Stephanie added. We all agreed. Mrs. Milton teaches 5A, and she's incredibly strict.

With all the talk about what our new *woman* teacher would be like, I was pretty surprised when I looked up and saw a young man standing by the door. He was tall, thin, and muscular-looking, and had wavy blond hair. To put it simply — he was gorgeous!

I saw Stephanie's jaw drop open! And we weren't the only ones who'd noticed him. All talking had stopped, and every girl in the room had her eyes practically glued to him.

"Hi, I'm your new science teacher," his deep voice boomed as he turned around to write "Mr. Talbot" on the board in huge letters. "We'll begin regular classes on Monday morning." His blond moustache wiggled when he spoke. "Please bring a brand-new notebook that you will use *only* for science. Also, I've ordered new textbooks, so Mrs. Mead will collect your old ones. In addition, I'll be assigning lab partners. We're going to be studying many different scientific methods, and I hope you'll enjoy exploring them as much as I'll enjoy teaching them." He smiled at us. I thought I heard Stephanie sigh.

Mrs. Mead appeared at the door. "Come in. They're all yours," Mr. Talbot said to her.

"Thanks, Quincy," she smiled. Then Mrs. Mead looked at the class. "After that brief orientation, I'm sure you're all excited about your new science lab. Now please line up quietly and walk back to 5B."

"That was it?" Kate complained as we got out of our chairs. "We hardly missed any social studies at all!"

"It was definitely worth seeing that man for any

amount of time!" Stephanie said as she stared back at Mr. Talbot.

When we got back to 5B, we had just enough time before the three o'clock bell rang to take a spelling test. All the words on that week's test were related to the science lab — stuff like *goggles, microscope,* and *beaker.* I gave Kate the thumbs-up sign before Mrs. Mead read the first word. "This oughta be a cinch!" she said, grinning.

For once, Kate and I were pretty confident we'd ace the test. I could tell Stephanie and Patti felt the same way. Mrs. Mead had made us copy the words from the board the week before, and the four of us had been quizzing each other. I guess even though science isn't exactly our favorite subject — except for Patti — we thought the new lab might make science pretty interesting.

A few weeks before, the carpenters, plumbers, and painters had come to put the final touches on the extra room that had been added to the back of Riverhurst Elementary. At first, we were less than enthusiastic about the idea of a special room for science.

"Why couldn't they build something most kids would really like?" Stephanie had asked. "Like a fashion design center?" Stephanie is really into fashion. She even has her own style of dressing. She wears only black, red, and white. It goes great with her dark curly hair.

"Or a weight room!" I suggested.

Patti was all for the lab from the very beginning. "The lab might make science fun," she told us. "For one thing, it'll be fun to change classrooms — like for gym or music or art. Plus, they'll have to hire a brand-new teacher who knows a lot about science — especially how to make it really interesting!"

"Like when Uncle Nick taught us all those cool experiments you can do with stuff you already have around the house," Stephanie reminded us. Once when Patti's uncle was staying with her and her brother, Horace, he showed all of us how to do some really neat experiments — like create an explosion just by using vinegar, baking soda, and dish detergent.

Patti's face lit up like a light. "Exactly!" she agreed.

Eventually, Patti convinced us that a new science lab wasn't such a bad idea after all. And now that I'd seen the room set up with all the neat equipment, I was sure she was right! Besides, how could anything be bad with Mr. Talbot in it?

Just as Mrs. Mead read out the last word on the test, the bell rang to dismiss us for the day. "Please put your quizzes on my desk as you leave," she shouted over the end-of-the-week noise. "See you on Monday!"

The sleepover was at Kate's house that night. We met a little earlier than usual because her parents were dropping us off at the Pizza Palace while they took Kate's little sister, Melissa, and her friend to see *Teenage Space Warriors* at the mall. We'd already seen it, and even though Kate would have liked to see it again, we talked her out of it. The Pizza Palace definitely has the best pizza in Riverhurst, so it didn't take us long to convince her.

"Let's sit over there," Patti suggested, pointing to a booth in the back of the restaurant. That was fine with the rest of us, since it would be quieter. In addition to the fact that there are usually a lot of people there, the Pizza Palace has video game machines next to the entrance. They make a lot of racket, but not half as much noise as the boys playing them. That night there were some sixth-grade boys glued to the screens.

Stephanie definitely had something on her mind. "I think I may start liking science almost as much as

Patti does," she said, wiggling her eyebrows. "Thanks to Q.T. Pie!"

"Who?" Kate asked.

"Mr. Talbot, of course. Didn't you hear Mrs. Mead call him 'Quincy'?" she explained. "Quincy Talbot. . . . Q.T. — Q.T. Pie!"

"That's great, Stephanie!" I said, laughing. Patti and Kate nodded.

I wouldn't have minded talking more about our great-looking new science teacher, but watching the other people in the restaurant eat was making my mouth water. "Boy, am I hungry!" I told the others.

"What a surprise, Lauren," Kate said sarcastically. Stephanie pretended to faint from shock. Patti giggled at them. They like to tease me about my appetite, which I guess *is* pretty healthy. I'm hungry almost all the time but never gain weight, so they call me the Bottomless Pit.

We ordered a double-cheese meatball pizza and a pitcher of Dr Pepper. Then we spent the meal talking nonstop about Mr. Talbot. As we were about to leave, my eye caught an unpleasant sight. Christy Soames and Ginger Kinkaid walked into the restaurant. They're both in 5C. We've never really gotten along very well — ever since Ginger tried to break up the Sleepover Friends. Now Christy and Ginger are inseparable, and they always dress identically. Tonight was no exception. They had on leather high-top sneakers with baggy pants, and oversized shirts with tank tops underneath. Christy was in orange and yellow, and Ginger had on black and blue. I had to admit, they both looked really great.

"Look at Ginger's earrings," Stephanie said. "She must have about a hundred pairs. She never wears the same ones twice!"

Patti looked at Ginger. "They *are* neat," she said. "But Ginger has pierced ears. They don't make clip-on earrings like that." None of us have pierced ears, so we usually don't wear earrings.

Ginger and Christy pretended not to see us and sat at the booth right behind ours. We could overhear everything they said. "I'm going to study really hard for Quincy's class," Ginger told Christy. "I'll probably be a better student than those Quarks nerds." Ginger tilted her head back toward us as she finished her sentence. Obviously, she knew we were listening.

Kate rolled her eyes. *"Quincy?"* she whispered. "Give me a break!"

"Don't worry about them," I reassured Patti. "They just want to bug us." Patti smiled. At first, she had worried about kids making fun of her for being in the Quarks, but then she realized most people thought it was kind of neat.

Actually, Stephanie looked more worried than Patti. "I can't believe Ginger thinks *she* can impress Mr. Talbot!" she said indignantly. "Why would he care about Ginger Kinkaid?" I guess Stephanie hadn't realized until then that she wasn't the only girl interested in Q.T. Pie!

Chapter
2

Kate's parents drove us back to the Beekmans' house after dinner. Luckily, they had bought a mini-van a little while ago, so all of the Sleepover Friends, *plus* Mr. and Mrs. Beekman, Melissa, and her friend, could all fit in one car. Stephanie didn't talk very much on the way home. She was probably thinking about Ginger and working on one of her great plans to win Q.T. Pie over. She must have figured something out, because she perked up once we got to Kate's house.

"What do you guys want to do till 'Friday Night Chillers' starts?" Kate asked once we were all in her bedroom.

"How about fixing our hair up in different styles?" Stephanie suggested.

13

Kate didn't look like that's what she had in mind. She's sort of a no-fuss type. She has straight blonde hair, and her idea of a hairstyle is putting on a head-band. But I suspected Stephanie's idea might have something to do with her mission to win Mr. Talbot over, so I decided to help out.

"Why not," I shrugged, looking at the scraggly strands of hair hanging in front of my eyes. "There was a section on hairstyles in *Teen Topics* this month."

Stephanie shook her head. "Oh, those are all so young," she said. She pulled a magazine out of her bag. It was twice as thick as *Teen Topics,* and was called *Elegance*. "I was thinking more like this." She opened the magazine to a picture of a woman with a red-sequined evening gown, elbow-length gloves, and a diamond bracelet and necklace. Her hair was all piled on top of her head with little wisps coming out.

Patti looked at the magazine and scrunched her nose. "I think we'd better stick to the ones in *Teen Topics,*" she said. "They look easier."

Kate and I agreed. If we were going to do hair-dos, we might as well do them right. We asked Mrs. Beekman if we could borrow her hot rollers, hair-pins, and some ribbons, and got to work on each

14

other's "new look." A couple of times, Melissa peeked in. "Oooo! You guys look just like movie stars," she said sarcastically. But most of the time she left us alone.

By the end of the second horror movie, I was ready to agree with Melissa. I looked more like the Bride of Frankenstein than the models in the magazine. I guessed I'd have to be satisfied with the limp look. Stephanie wasn't ready to quit, though. She looked sort of like a poodle with her wavy black hair perched in tight curls on top of her head.

"Oh, this is so babyish," she complained.

"I have an idea," I suggested, trying to get Stephanie's mind on something else. "How about a game of Truth or Dare?"

"Yeah!" Kate and Patti cheered.

"I get to go first," Stephanie said. "I pick Patti."

Patti paused, then said, "I pick truth."

"Okay," Stephanie began. "Who would you rather look through a microscope with: Henry or Q.T. Pie?"

"That's easy — Mr. Talbot," she answered.

"Really?!" we all said.

"Henry would be a horrible science partner," Patti explained. "He wouldn't know the difference between fungus and algae." We all groaned, disappointed that she'd been so reasonable about her choice — especially since *we* didn't know the difference between fungus and algae either!

Kate asked me my question. "If you could share a Charlie's Double-Sundae Surprise with either Kevin DeSpain or Quincy, who would you pick?"

"Well . . . probably Quincy Talbot," I hesitated. "But he seems more like the carrot juice type. Did you see those biceps? I bet he's a great athlete!"

Almost every question in the rest of the game had something to do with Q.T. Pie. Of course, Stephanie *always* mentioned him in her answer. No doubt about it — Quincy Talbot was the best thing to happen to Truth or Dare since Stephanie's crush on Taylor Sprouse! Even after we'd finished the game and put on our pajamas, we continued to talk about him. Patti was happy the Quarks wouldn't have to go to the university anymore for equipment. Kate thought he seemed fair and organized. Stephanie, of course, couldn't get her mind off his great looks! I thought he was really great-looking, too, but I was just as happy to have a teacher who I hoped would make science interesting!

I woke up late Monday morning and had to dress in a hurry. I had stayed up late the night before reading my old science textbook, getting ready for our first class with Mr. Talbot. Unfortunately, I didn't have enough time to pick out something nice to wear. I kind of wanted Mr. Talbot to notice me, but Stephanie always looks so good, I knew there was really no use in my trying. Next to her, I always look like I've gotten dressed with my eyes closed. And, next to Patti, I certainly wouldn't get his attention with my grades.

I was about to give up and race out the door when I noticed my red baseball cap lying on my desk. That was it. Mr. Talbot looked like he was in really good shape. He was probably an athlete. I'd help him realize how much we have in common!

I put the cap on my head, grabbed a banana and a slice of toast, and raced down our long driveway on my bike. I have to ride farther than the others to get to our morning meeting place, and that morning I was really late.

As I pedaled up the hill to our corner, Stephanie caught my eye long before I was even within shouting distance! Her hair was pulled up on top of her head in a loose ponytail. She had on an oversized red T-shirt that she'd designed and painted with black-and-white paint squiggles, belted at the waist over black pants. But what really stood out were her earrings! They were shaped just like nacho chips — and Mexican food is my favorite!

Kate must have noticed my staring. "You'd better watch out, Stephanie!" she warned when I reached the top of the hill. "Lauren may try to eat your ears!"

After we stopped giggling and started riding toward school, I said, "You look great, Steph! What's the occasion?"

Stephanie looked down at her black-and-red-checkered handlebars. "Oh . . . nothing," she said breezily.

Patti grinned. "It wouldn't have anything to do with a certain science teacher, would it?" she asked.

"It might," Stephanie said slyly. Then she looked at me suspiciously. "What's with the baseball cap, Lauren? Trying to look a little athletic?"

We all cracked up. Usually, the only times I wear the cap are when I'm playing baseball or trying to hide a hairstyling disaster. And the Sleepover Friends knew it!

"I have an idea," Stephanie said. "I was thinking that Mr. Talbot might want me and some other kids to paint a mural on the science lab wall. You know . . . like we did in the art studio." Stephanie's a really great artist. She and a bunch of other kids painted a huge picture on Ms. Gilberto's art room wall. Stephanie even drew the Sleepover Friends sitting at our usual lunch table!

"That's a good idea," I agreed. "You could draw trees and plants."

"Or portraits of famous scientists," Patti added, even though she was probably the only one who knew the names of many scientists, let alone what they looked like!

"Even if I don't get a great grade, at least he'll know how important I think science is," Stephanie said.

Kate looked Stephanie up and down and rolled her eyes. "Don't you mean he'll know how important you think *fashion* is?" Kate said.

"And gorgeous men!" I laughed.

After Mrs. Mead took attendance, we went straight to science lab. And everyone else was as excited as the Sleepover Friends.

"I hope we get to build skeletons," Pete said as we walked down the hall.

"I don't care what Mr. Talbot teaches us as long as he's the one teaching it," Jenny Carlin said. I like Jenny even less than Ginger and Christy. She's a complete phony. Unfortunately, I think that just about every girl in the class agreed at least a little bit with her.

The laboratory looked pretty much the same as it had the week before — except there were white pieces of paper with names written on them on each desk, and brand-new science books next to them.

Everyone milled around looking for the right seat, and Mr. Talbot announced, "Please find your assigned seats quickly so that we can get started."

I was pretty happy when I saw Mark Freedman's name on the desk next to mine. He teases the Sleepover Friends a lot, but he's not nasty about it or anything. Right across from me was Jane Sykes, who wasn't quite as lucky as I was when it came to partners. Hers was David Degan. Unlike Mark, just about everything David says is mean. I thought about our game of Truth or Dare the Friday before. I was just happy I didn't have to share a microscope with him!

Patti got lucky, too. She and her lab partner, Hope Lenski, were sitting at the next table talking and smiling. They're a great match. Hope's pretty new to Riverhurst, and she's the only person I know who's as nice as Patti.

Patti and Hope shared a table with Pete and Kate, who were talking, although I'm not sure what they could have been talking about. The only thing Pete likes is baseball, and Kate isn't the least bit interested in that!

Then I looked over at Stephanie, who was sitting right next to Mr. Talbot's desk. She had her chin in her hand, and she looked upset. Her lab partner was Jenny! And across from her sat Jenny's sidekick, Angela Kemp, and Karla Stamos, the class grind. Karla already had her nose deep in the new science book.

"All right," Mr. Talbot began. "It looks as though everyone has found a seat, so I'll take attendance."

"Don't worry," Henry spoke up. "Mrs. Mead already did."

"I'm not worried, Henry," Mr. Talbot said, smiling. "I'd just like to get to know everyone a little better."

Henry looked stunned. "Hey," he cried out. "How'd you know my name?" The whole class cracked up — especially Patti. I guess Henry's reputation was a lot bigger than he suspected!

But Mr. Talbot seemed to know something about almost everybody. When he called Patti's name, he said, "I understand you're in Quarks. I may need your help demonstrating for the class." Patti blushed.

And after I responded "Here," he said, "Mrs.

21

Mead tells me you're quite an athlete." So I didn't have to wear the baseball cap after all!

He had a comment for everyone. Even if he didn't know something about someone, he'd say, "It's nice to meet you." And he told Hope she has a pretty name — which she does.

Once he'd finished, Mr. Talbot picked up a piece of chalk and turned to face the chalkboard. In capital letters, he wrote LABORATORY RULES. We slowly copied them:

1. *Always wear a smock.*
2. *Always wear goggles during chemistry experiments.*
3. *No horseplay.*

Suddenly Mr. Talbot's booming voice interrupted our scribbling. "Excuse me. You're squinting. Are you having difficulty seeing, Kate?" he called to the back of the room.

"Well . . . yes . . . a little," Kate said hesitantly. "I usually sit in the second row." I felt sorry for her. Kate is supposed to wear glasses all the time, but she hardly ever does. She hates to be reminded about them, and Mr. Talbot was reminding her in front of the whole class.

Mr. Talbot pointed to Jenny. "Why don't you change places with her, please," he instructed. Jenny grabbed her name card and notebook, hopped out of her chair, and slid into the seat next to Pete. She had a completely idiotic grin on her face. It was sickening to see how excited she was to sit next to him.

Kate grinned, too, and quietly slipped into the seat next to Stephanie, as Mr. Talbot continued writing on the board.

Things couldn't have gone better. Mr. Talbot wasn't overly nice like Ms. Gilberto, but he didn't seem to be mean either. After we had finished copying the rules in our notebooks, he explained the types of science we'd be studying: biology and chemistry. Cool! Just like in high school! I know, because my brother, Roger, is seventeen and has taken both of them.

Next, Mr. Talbot handed out a schedule for the class, which he called a "syllabus." "Some of you may want to work ahead, so I'm letting you know what we'll be doing for the rest of the year," he explained. "As you can see, we'll start by studying the animal kingdom and the differences between the species. To prepare for class tomorrow, please read the first chapter in your new book on dissection. We'll be dissecting some animals that are very similar to humans, and some that are very different."

"Ooooh!" Jenny's shriek rang loud and clear up to the front of the room.

Not everyone was distressed by the news, though. "All right!" David Degan cheered. "Will the animals be alive?"

I could tell Mr. Talbot didn't appreciate the remark. "Dissection is an important diagnostic tool that teaches human beings about themselves and other animals," he replied sternly. "A scientist's purpose is to enlighten, *not* to harm. The moment you step through that door in the morning, you have to begin thinking like a scientist."

By the time Mr. Talbot finished his lecture, David was slumped down in his chair with a bright red face.

I still couldn't believe my ears! I looked down at the syllabus. Right there next to the following day's date was the word *dissection*. Just thinking about it was making me uneasy.

"This week we'll begin the procedure, but today I want to introduce you to the equipment," he told us. One by one, he held up the dissection instruments: a wax plate, pins, a scalpel. . . . Even though he wasn't actually doing anything with them, I started to feel kind of sick to my stomach.

"And, finally, we'll be using frogs." Mr. Talbot

talked as though frogs were no more alive than our microscopes! I thought about all the creepy-crawlies Patti's little brother, Horace, keeps in the Jenkins' basement. He has two frogs, and he even let us name one: Freda! How could I even *think* about experimenting on her?

Mr. Talbot looked at his watch. "It looks like we've run out of time," he said cheerfully. "Please learn the safety rules, read the chapter, and come to class tomorrow prepared."

I was in such a daze as I walked out of the room that I dropped my science book on the floor. Mr. Talbot bent over to pick it up. "Better not do that in a ball game." He smiled. I had a lot of trouble smiling back. How could a man who seemed so nice want us to hurt innocent frogs?

Chapter 3

I thought about science class the rest of the morning. I couldn't wait to talk to my friends at lunch. I wanted to know how they felt about the dissection.

Stephanie was the last one to sit down. "Did you guys hear the way Q.T. Pie said, 'It's nice to meet you' to me this morning?" she bubbled. "I could have died!"

"He said that to everyone, Steph," Kate said, shaking her head.

Patti's eyes twinkled. "He even noticed that Lauren's an athlete."

But I was still preoccupied with the dissection. "What do you guys think about dissecting a frog?" I asked. "I mean, isn't it kind of weird thinking that frogs can be something besides pets? When I think

26

of frogs, I think of the ones Roger and I used to catch down by Munn's Pond, or the ones Horace keeps in your basement, Patti."

Stephanie scrunched up her nose. She may have helped name Freda, but she definitely was not her biggest fan.

Kate was the first to say something. "I guess so," she answered thoughtfully. "But frogs aren't like cats or dogs. We would never use *them* for science class." We felt that way because we don't have any pet frogs, but I was willing to bet that Horace's frogs were as important to him as my dog, Bullwinkle, or my cat, Rocky, were to me.

"When we dissected a worm in Quarks, Mr. Murdock told us we had to think of it scientifically," Patti said, putting down her fork. "He said emotions shouldn't get in the way of science."

"Maybe he's right," I said, but I still wasn't sure.

"I hope you're not thinking about telling Q.T. that you don't want to do the dissection," Stephanie said with a concerned look on her face.

"I haven't decided," I told her.

"Everybody else is going to — it's not like you have a choice, Lauren," Stephanie started to sound worried. "Next you'll be trying to get out of English tests."

"I don't think that's what she's trying to do." Patti quickly came to my defense, trying to head off an argument.

"I'm sure Mrs. Mead told him we're best friends," Stephanie told Patti and Kate. "He's going to think we're all troublemakers." Then she looked directly at me. "Besides, Mr. Talbot wouldn't make us do anything that would hurt animals!"

I didn't want to talk about the dissection anymore. Stephanie wanted to protect Mr. Talbot as much as I wanted to protect the frogs. But it wasn't worth upsetting my best friends when I hadn't even decided what to do. Besides, Hope had sat down with us. She's in Quarks, too, so I was sure that she would feel the same way as Patti.

Hope pulled an alfalfa-and-avocado-on-pita sandwich out of her lunch bag. I hadn't even heard of alfalfa until I met Hope. She's a vegetarian, so she eats stuff like that all the time.

"I guess everyone's pretty excited about the science lab," she said, not really sounding as cheerful as she usually did.

"Of course," Stephanie responded immediately. "Who wouldn't be, with Q.T. Pie teaching?"

Patti grinned. "It's also really great for the Quarks," she added. "Now we can do interesting experiments without going all the way to the university."

"Yeah," Hope said. "I guess there are a lot of good things about it." I wasn't sure why, but I had a feeling that Hope didn't really believe that.

That night, the only thing I had to do before my mom and dad got home from work was to put the tuna bake in the oven and make a salad. Mom always prepares the main dish the night before, so when Roger and I get home, we don't have to do anything really tough. And I'd made so many salads, I could tear lettuce in my sleep. After I got dinner ready, I went to my bedroom and shut the door. I didn't want anyone — or anything, especially our 130-pound Newfoundland, Bullwinkle — to bother me. I needed to concentrate on the assigned chapter in my science book.

I didn't feel too enthusiastic about reading the chapter, so I flipped to the back of the book first. There were a lot of really colorful drawings and photographs with different kinds of plants and animals. I kept thinking that if I could just learn about those things, I would really like science. I knew, though, that I was just avoiding the inevitable. Eventually, I would have to read the assignment.

Maybe once I'd read it, I'd see that Mr. Talbot and Patti were right after all, and then all my troubles would be over. Maybe if I saw the explanation and the pictures of what was inside the dissected animals, I'd see that dissection really did serve a purpose. Maybe I only felt funny about it because nobody had really explained what that purpose was.

Once I finally opened to the first page of the book, I bet I read every sentence at least three times, and looked at each picture for about five minutes. It seemed so strange to think that the frogs and worms in the pictures were just like the ones I would experiment on the next day — or worst of all, just like Horace's pets!

After I finished reading, I was just as confused as I had been before I started. The chapter explained *how* to do everything, but not *whether* to do it. Maybe that's what was bothering me most. Everyone just assumed there was nothing wrong with a bunch of kids examining the insides of animals.

But every time I felt like I was beginning to sort things out, I began to doubt myself again. The science book was written by scientists. Patti wanted to be a scientist, and Mr. Talbot was a scientist. They all thought dissection was okay. I've always thought it was really important to listen to experts because you

30

can learn a lot from them. So if all the experts believed that dissecting frogs was okay, it must be — right?

I didn't bring up the lab during dinner. It might be okay to talk about it at lunch with the Sleepover Friends, but stuff like dissection is definitely *off-limits* at my family's dinner table! I guess my mom could tell something was wrong, though, because she kept saying, "You ate only one small serving of tuna, honey." To anyone who knows me, that's just not normal.

I didn't talk very much while my dad and I cleared the table. He tried to ask me about school, but that was the last thing I wanted to talk about.

After we finished loading the last plate into the dishwasher, I went back to my room and stayed there most of the night — even though a special episode of *Made for Each Other* was on at eight o'clock. The phone rang right at eight-thirty, so I stepped into the hall to pick it up. I was ready for a break anyway. I grabbed the receiver on the second ring.

"Hi, Lauren." I heard Patti's voice on the other end. "Weren't Kevin and Marcy great tonight? That was definitely the best episode so far!" Marcy Monroe is Kevin DeSpain's co-star on the show.

"Uh . . ." I hesitated. "I didn't see it."

"Why not?" Patti asked. "It's your favorite."

"Well . . . um . . . I was doing homework," I told her, feeling a little guilty that I wasn't exactly telling the truth. Ever since dinner, I'd been in my room lying on the floor. (Actually I was lying on a layer of clothes. My room's always pretty messy.)

"Oh," she said. I was pretty sure she could tell something was wrong. I usually wouldn't miss my favorite TV show to do homework. And Patti knew it!

"I guess I'd better go now," I said.

"Okay." She tried to sound cheerful. "See you tomorrow!"

About an hour later, my parents tapped on my door. "Your dad and I are pretty tired. We're going to bed early. Will you be up much longer, honey?" Mom asked.

I forced a smile. "I'll probably just read a couple more articles in *Star Turns*," I told her. *Star Turns* is one of my favorite magazines. I didn't want to tell them that I had too much on my mind to fall asleep.

"Don't forget to turn out the hall light before you fall asleep," Dad reminded me. They went into their bedroom and shut the door behind them.

I tried to read a little of my magazine, but kept

getting distracted. I turned on WBRM and sang along to Heat's newest song, but even "Crazy Love" couldn't make me forget about the science lab.

There was no way I could do the dissection, but how could I avoid it? It wouldn't be fair to make Mark do all the icky work while I just sat there doing nothing. Besides, I didn't even want to be in the same room while everyone else was dissecting!

There was only one thing I could do: I had to think of some way to get out of science. Maybe I could say I was allergic to frogs! No, that wouldn't work. They'd ask me to bring in a note from my mother, and I couldn't ask her to lie for me just because I was grossed out by the thought of dissecting a frog.

Roger must have seen the light on under my door when he got in. He and his girlfriend, Linda, had gone to a movie. "Hey, Squirt," he said as he tapped on my door. "You still up?" He cracked the door a little and peeked in.

"Yeah, I guess I'm not really tired," I told him.

"Come on. You can't fool me," he said in a suspicious tone. "There are probably three Sleepover Friends huddled under your bed, ready to terrorize some fifth-grade boy as soon as I fall asleep. I think I even smell Alaska dip." Each of the Sleepover

Friends has a specialty, and Alaska dip is Patti's.

As far as older brothers go, Roger's not so bad. He usually knows how to cheer me up — even if it's just a little bit. "Actually, Roger, they're hiding there to terrorize *you*!" I giggled. "I wouldn't fall asleep if I were you!" I twisted my face like a monster, and Roger left to go to his room.

It would have been great to have had the Sleep-over Friends right there, I thought. But I knew that if I looked under the mattress, the only thing I'd see would be dust bunnies and dirty socks!

I tossed and turned most of the night, trying to decide how to face Mr. Talbot, my parents, and the Sleepover Friends the next day. What would they think if I said there was no way I could participate in the dissection? Would I be punished? Would I have to repeat fifth-grade science over and over until I finally gave in? Would my best friends ever speak to me again? Finally, I fell asleep, but I kept waking up worried about the same thing.

When the alarm clock rang the next morning, I had finally figured out a foolproof plan: I'd stay home from school. By the end of the day, I wouldn't have a problem anymore!

I went downstairs and told my mother I couldn't go to school because I wasn't feeling well.

"Yes, Roger said you were up late. I was afraid you might not be feeling well," she said sympathetically and felt my forehead. "You don't feel warm. Does your stomach hurt?"

I tried to look tired and pathetic, which wasn't too hard since I'd been up most of the night worrying. "Y-y-yeah," I nodded. "My stomach's bothering me." It wasn't exactly a lie. Every time I thought about a poor little frog lying on its back on my lab table, my stomach did a somersault.

Besides, it wasn't like I was staying home just for myself. It was for the frog, too. I owed it to frogs everywhere to stay home!

My mother bent over and kissed me on the cheek. "I'll come home on my lunch hour and make sure you're okay," she said. "You'd better go back to bed." I would have preferred curling up in front of the TV, but even being confined to my bed all day was better than going to science lab!

I started to read the English homework for the next day. I didn't get very far, though, because Rocky came into my room and hopped up on my bed. He must have known I was feeling rotten because he tried to comfort me by curling up on my lap and licking my hands. I really wanted to play with him outside. It was a really sunny day. But I knew my mom would be upset with me if I didn't stay in bed.

By the time my mother came home at noon, I had a first-class case of cabin fever. I kept wondering what the Sleepover Friends were doing and if they missed me.

"I brought you some tomato soup and crackers from Deli Delights to make your stomach feel better," my mother said, putting the tray of food on my desk.

I couldn't stand it anymore! Mom was being so nice, and I was feeling super-guilty. I had to tell her why I'd stayed home. "Well . . ." I hesitated. "Actually, my stomach feels a lot better now. Um . . . when you were in school, did you ever have to dissect anything in science class?"

I hadn't told her about our assignment, so she wasn't exactly sure what I was talking about. But I could tell by the "ah-ha" expression on her face that she had a pretty good idea. "When I was in college, I did," she said. "In biology we had to dissect a cockroach," she explained.

Ugh! Gross! I didn't know anyone who had a pet roach, but that didn't sound any easier than dissecting a frog. "So you think it's all right for me to do a dissection in science?" I asked.

My mom didn't actually answer me. "What's all

right for me, Lauren, may not be all right for you," she said.

"In science this morning, we were each supposed to dissect a frog," I told her. "I guess I stayed home because I didn't want to do it."

I expected Mom to be angry at me for skipping school, but instead of being mad, she looked pretty sympathetic. She put her hand on top of mine. "When I was in school, nobody really thought about whether or not it was okay," she said. I couldn't imagine my mother not caring about hurting animals. "But now there are other ways to do a lot of things that people my age didn't have. Like using a computer to help simulate a dissection without actually having to use real animals. Or using animal models that look and feel like real animals."

"What about just reading my book?" I asked. "There's a whole chapter about dissection. It was kind of gross to look at the animals and know that they were once real, but I learned a lot about the similarities and differences between people and animals." In a way, I was beginning to understand things better. But I was still really confused. "So why don't we use the other ways?" I asked her.

"Well . . . some people believe that the way

we've always done it is the best way," she explained. "They learned about animals by using dissection, so they think everyone else should. Maybe using one of the new ways *wouldn't* teach us as much. And maybe you can learn more by actually doing the dissecting than you can just by reading about it." She looked at her watch. "Oh, I've got to get back to the office," she said in a panicked voice. "Let me know if you need anything. I'll be home at the usual time."

When my mother left, I realized I still didn't have any answers to my questions. I'd already missed the class, but should I have gone through with it? I still didn't know why the idea of dissection made me feel so sick. And did the Sleepover Friends think I'd let them down?

Chapter
4

At three o'clock that afternoon, I felt really relieved. School was over, and I'd managed to avoid the dissection. I did have a few guilt pangs about my friends having to go through it while I chickened out, but I was confident I'd done the right thing by staying home.

The phone rang at 3:10 — just about the time Kate, Stephanie, and Patti would be getting home. I quickly picked up the phone, happy I could talk to them again. "Hi," Stephanie's voice boomed through the receiver. "We're in my apartment. Are you feeling better?" Stephanie's parents built a great playroom for her in the Greens' backyard. Stephanie likes to call it an apartment because she thinks it sounds mature.

"Uh . . . yeah . . . I feel great!" I said cheerfully. *Relieved* was more like it! "How was school?"

"Pretty boring," she said. "Q.T. Pie gave us a pop quiz on the chapter we were supposed to have read. Then we went to art and lunch, and Mrs. Mead showed a film. . . ." I tuned out as Stephanie told me about the rest of their day, and the sick feeling in my stomach came back.

"Hi, Lauren." Kate's voice brought me back to reality. Kate's pretty good at that. "Patti said you sounded crummy last night. Sorry."

"Did Q.T. have you dissect frogs after the quiz?" I asked.

"No. He wanted to make sure we understood everything first," Kate explained.

"Patti wants to know if you want us to come over." Stephanie passed the message to me.

"No," I groaned. "I have a feeling I wouldn't be much fun to be around." We said good-bye and hung up the phone.

I was feeling miserable again. *Now* what would I do?! I couldn't pretend to be sick again. I had already confessed to my mom. Even though she didn't get mad at me that afternoon, I knew she wouldn't let me stay home another day. There was only one thing to do. I had already tried taking the easy way out. Now it was time to face Quincy Talbot!

The next morning, I bicycled to meet Kate, Stephanie, and Patti at our usual corner. Again, I had stayed up most of the night before, so I was moving pretty slowly. But since I couldn't sleep, I'd had a lot of time to think about what I was going to do. And I had decided to tell the others my plan.

"Hurry up," Stephanie shouted at me. "We don't want to be late!" I did. This could turn out to be the worst day of my life. But I knew what Stephanie meant. If you're late more than once, you have to spend lunch in Mrs. Wainwright's office. Of course, that might be small potatoes compared to my fate if I refused to dissect a frog!

As I got closer, huffing and puffing, Patti, Kate, and Stephanie started pedaling as fast as they could. "We thought you were sick again," Kate said, hunched over her handlebars. "I mean, you were even later than usual! One more minute and we would have left."

"Sorry," I apologized as I followed behind the others. "I guess I had a little trouble getting moving this morning."

"We'll make it on time," Patti reassured us.

She was right — we made it *just* in time! The late bell rang as I stepped through the door behind the others.

I handed Mrs. Mead the excuse my mother had written for me to get back into class. "I'm glad to see you're feeling better today, Lauren — even if you girls are cutting it a little close this morning," she said.

I hadn't had a chance to tell the others about my plan not to do the dissection. So, in addition to not knowing how Mr. Talbot would react, I had no idea how my three best friends would react!

But the worst part was that there was practically no way I could avoid making at least a small scene in the lab. I mean, I couldn't exactly march up to Q.T. Pie and say, "May I please see you out in the hall, Mr. Talbot?" He'd probably laugh me all the way to Mrs. Wainwright's office!

Mrs. Mead lined us up, and we walked down the hall to the science lab. Stephanie turned around in line. "You still look really sick, Lauren," she whispered. "Maybe you should've stayed home another day." She was definitely right about that. I figured I should probably stay home the rest of the year. After what I was planning to do, I might *have* to!

I just smiled weakly at Stephanie. I was so nervous, even if I had tried to talk, I would have needed help prying my mouth open. I could barely move enough to walk down the hall, and the closer I got to the science lab, the worse I felt.

I snapped out of it, though, when I heard strange squealing noises from the back of the line. "I know I'll get sick. Just the thought of it makes me feel queasy. I tried to pretend to be sick, but my mom wouldn't let me." Someone else felt exactly like I did! But it didn't make me feel any better when I spun around and realized it was Jenny Carlin! Just what I needed, to have something in common with Miss Priss. I hadn't been at school more than ten minutes, and this was already the worst day of my life!

"Don't worry, Jenny," Larry Jackson smirked. "The frog's just as afraid of you as you are of it!" He stuck his tongue way out and distorted his face. For the first time ever, Jenny couldn't come up with one of her not-so-clever comebacks.

I had an idea. What if I waited and didn't say anything to Mr. Talbot right away? Maybe Jenny would say something to him, and we could both get out of it. But Jenny immediately shattered my hopes. She turned to Angela and whined — just as loudly as she had squealed — "But Mr. Talbot is so gorgeous, how can I tell him I don't want to do his assignment?" I guessed *I* would have to be the one to lead the SAVE THE FROG Crusade!

My legs were shaking, but somehow I managed to make it to the lab. Q.T. Pie was standing by the classroom door, smiling and greeting every student.

"I'm glad you're back, Lauren," he said as I walked past. "We missed our star athlete yesterday." Mr. Talbot was really nice.

"Gosh," I said softly, finally able to speak. "Maybe he'll understand."

"Understand what?" Kate scrunched up her face. "You've hardly said anything this morning."

"Oh . . . uh . . . understand why I didn't take the quiz yesterday," I said without thinking.

"I'm sure he'll understand. Next to Mr. Murdock, he's the best science teacher I've ever had," Patti said, walking to her seat.

Mr. Talbot cleared his throat. "On the whole, you all did very well on your quizzes." He smiled. "Those of you who got a C or below will be quizzed on the material again Tuesday." Then he looked directly at me. "Lauren, you may join the others today in the dissection, and take the make-up quiz on Tuesday."

The whole time Mr. Talbot was looking at me, though, I had my eye on something else. Three buckets were sitting on his lab table, and I had a sickening feeling I knew what was in them! Without even thinking, I blurted out, "Do I have to do the dissection?"

"Lauren!" Stephanie screeched. "What are you talking about?"

"I mean," I began more quietly, "I really don't want to do the dissection."

Mr. Talbot remained calm. "Why not?" he asked.

"I just don't think we should use frogs for science class," I explained. Then I thought for a second. "Unless . . . did they die from natural causes — like old age?"

Mr. Talbot ignored the whispering in the back of the classroom. "No, Lauren. Actually, these frogs were raised in special labs so they could be used just for this purpose," he explained. "They weren't taken out of a pond or anyone's home. And they died painlessly: They inhaled poisonous gases."

I was dying of embarrassment. Stephanie tried to help me out. "She was really sick yesterday," she explained frantically and looked at Mr. Talbot. "She's *delirious*!"

Kate put her finger to her lips and shushed Stephanie.

"I still can't do it." I stood firm. "They're animals!"

"You're being too emotional," Mr. Talbot said firmly. "Part of being a good scientist is putting emotions aside . . . and sometimes doing things we'd rather not do." Was he accusing me of trying to get out of doing the work? I guess it looked pretty bad. First, I had missed the quiz, and now I was trying to skip the lab. How was I going to convince him?

Patti gave me a sympathetic look. Maybe Mr. Talbot was right. Maybe part of being a good scientist was forgetting about emotions. After all, Patti is the nicest person I know, and she'd done a dissection.

Finally, I breathed in all the air I possibly could and let it back out. "Okay," I said quickly. "I'll try!"

Stephanie breathed a loud sigh of relief. I heard it all the way over at my table. "Way to go, Lauren," Mark whispered. "You can do it!"

Mr. Talbot gave each set of partners a frog. He explained how to pin the frog down so that we could see its stomach. "I'll do it," Mark volunteered, trying to help me get through it.

"Gross!" Jenny said. "What's that smell?" This was getting scary — Jenny and I were starting to think alike. I was curious about the strong odor, too.

"That's formaldehyde," Mr. Talbot responded. "It preserves the bodies." Preserves the bodies? For what? Why did we have to go to so much trouble to raise the animals a special way, kill them, preserve them, and then cut them up? The more I thought about it, the less sense it made.

Mr. Talbot went on to talk about where to make the incisions, what to look for inside the frog, and how it did or didn't relate to the human body. My head started spinning, and my stomach felt out of control, too. I knew I wouldn't be able to listen much longer without getting sick!

Finally, I jumped out of my chair. "I just can't do it!" I cried. I couldn't believe it. Before, I had been afraid of making a scene, and there I was, openly defying a teacher — our brand-new teacher. The worst part was that everyone — except the Sleepover Friends, Hope, Jenny, and Angela — was laughing at me. The Sleepover Friends and Hope I could understand . . . but Jenny and Angela? They were usually only too happy to give me a hard time.

"Please, Lauren," Mr. Talbot's voice still sounded kind. "Can't you just try? You must approach this like a scientist." The problem was that I *was* thinking like a scientist. I had researched the subject, read about it, and considered all the alternatives. I had even tried to consider how it would benefit me. But I just couldn't stop thinking about the frog.

"I'm sorry, Mr. Talbot," I apologized as I sat back down next to Mark. "I can't."

"Mrs. Mead told me you're a good student, Lauren," he explained. "But unless you do this lab, you can't possibly get a good grade in science."

Suddenly grades weren't the most important thing. I hung my head. "I know," I agreed.

"And I'll have to ask your parents to come in for a conference about this," he said. Oh, no! How would my parents feel if they knew I had refused to do what a teacher had asked? But there was just no way I was backing down now.

"Okay," I mumbled, embarrassed that everyone's attention was focused on me.

"Please take your chair and science book out in the hall and read for the rest of the period," he told me. I got up from my desk completely humiliated. I had gotten in trouble before — but it was never this bad. And I knew that even if I *did* end up doing the dissection because my parents made me, there was no way Mr. Talbot would ever be nice to me again.

Chapter
5

I'd barely had enough time to put my chair down, open my book, and start reading before Hope followed me into the hall with *her* chair.

"What are you doing?" I asked.

"I guess I wasn't cut out to be a scientist, either," she shrugged.

"But that's not true," I protested. "You're really good in science. You're in Quarks. Why aren't you doing the dissection?"

"Because I think it's the wrong thing to do," she explained.

"But what if the experts are right? What if dissection *is* the only way we can learn about science?" I wondered aloud.

"What experts, Lauren?" she asked, getting a

little excited. "My dad never had to hurt a single animal to learn about them, and he's the best doctor I know." Her father's a veterinarian. "It just wouldn't make sense."

Well, it finally made sense to me! *If Hope's father could learn enough about animals to care for them without dissecting a single one, why should fifth-graders have to dissect them at all?* I thought. They *shouldn't* have to if it's not completely necessary.

I had cleared up the dissection issue, but now I was confused about Hope. "At lunch the other day, you said there were a lot of good things about lab," I reminded her.

"I still think there are," she agreed. "Once we get past the dissection, it'll be great!"

It was a relief finally to be able to talk to someone who knew exactly how I felt. "Why didn't you say something to Q.T., uh, Mr. Talbot, sooner?" I asked her.

Hope hung her head a little. "I'm still the newcomer around here," she said shyly. "You know how hard it was for me to make friends when I first moved here. Everyone thought I was so different. They're finally starting to accept me. So I guess I was afraid to speak up."

A lot of people *did* think Hope was really weird when she first moved to Riverhurst. She has hair all the way down her back that she twists into lots of tiny braids, and she dresses in unusual clothes made out of wild prints. But once the Sleepover Friends got to know her, we discovered what a great person she is. And now I was more convinced than ever.

Hope and I sat outside and talked quietly until the kids started coming out of the science lab. Then we got up and walked with them back to 5B. I could see the questions on my friends' faces, but there wasn't enough time to talk about things. Everyone knew it would be better to wait until we had a chance later on to discuss what had happened.

We had independent reading after science. Mrs. Mead watches us like a hawk, and one whisper or note could be big trouble — like a visit to Mrs. Wainwright's office! And I wasn't about to get in any more trouble than I was probably already in, so I had to wait until lunch to find out how the Sleepover Friends felt about the scene I'd caused.

Stephanie, Kate, and Patti were all sitting at our usual lunch table, waiting for me, which I figured was a pretty good sign. It looked like they still wanted to eat lunch with me. Or at least that's what I thought until Stephanie noticed me, looked down at her

51

plate, and started scooping forkfuls of spaghetti and meatballs into her mouth.

"Wow, Lauren," Patti said, stabbing a french fry with her fork. "What you did in Mr. Talbot's class took a lot of guts."

"Do you really think so?" I said. "You're not mad? It must have looked like I was saying everyone else was wrong for doing the dissection."

"Well . . . " she said thoughtfully. "I don't agree with you. I think the benefits to scientists outweigh the cost to the animals. But I think you were right to stick up for what you believe."

"Besides, a lot of kids feel the way you do," Kate added. "They just didn't speak up."

That *really* got my attention. "Like who?" I asked.

Kate leaned forward. "Jenny and Angela couldn't do it, so they had to watch their science partners and take notes. Angela almost fainted, though, so Q.T. Pie told her to read her science book for the rest of the class."

"Even David Degan thought it was completely sickening," Patti said. "He had to sit with his head between his knees!"

Stephanie shot Kate and Patti a nasty glance. "I don't see why you're making such a big deal out of

52

this, Lauren," she said sternly. "Q.T. Pie's new, and you're just making trouble. Now he definitely won't like our class! He probably thinks we agree with you because we hang around together!" Stephanie's always pretty outspoken, but I could tell that she was really mad at me.

"If Mr. Talbot's such a good teacher," Kate said, "he shouldn't judge people based on their friends. Besides, even though I did the dissection, I think Lauren's right!"

Stephanie looked really angry. "Fine!" she yelled. "But I won't worry about what Mr. Talbot thinks of my friends anymore, because as far as I'm concerned, you're not my friend!"

"Fine!" Kate said.

"Fine!" Stephanie said back. Then she picked up her tray and stalked to a table at the opposite end of the lunchroom.

Patti and I sat there stunned as Kate hunched over her sandwich. Had *I* done this to the Sleepover Friends? I couldn't even finish my lunch.

"Don't worry," Patti whispered to me. "They'll probably patch things up by the end of the day."

Unfortunately, Patti was wrong. Stephanie sits right in front of me and Kate in Mrs. Mead's class, but she didn't turn around to talk to us the entire day! And instead of riding home together on our bikes like we usually do, Stephanie ran out of 5B and hopped on her bike before Patti or I could say anything.

Kate walked out with me and Patti, but rode off quickly. I rode home in silence with Patti, completely miserable. The Sleepover Friends had had troubles before, but it was usually because of some sort of misunderstanding. This time there was no misunderstanding — just a huge disagreement!

Suddenly, Patti looked as if a light bulb had gone on in her head. "I have an idea!" she said happily. "Come over to my house at around five o'clock. I'll tell Kate and Stephanie to come over, too." Then she gave me a sly look. "But I won't tell them everybody else will be there."

"Excellent idea!" I agreed. "It'll be just like an emergency meeting — only they won't know it!" Usually, emergency meetings are called so that we can get organized — like the time Kate won tickets to Wilderness World in a raffle, but she didn't win enough for all of us to go! We had to call an emergency meeting to figure out a way to raise enough money for an extra ticket.

But this was the biggest emergency we'd ever had. And it was all my fault.

It was Roger's turn to get dinner that night, so after he put the roast beef in the oven, I asked him to drive me over to Patti's. "Sure, I'll take you on my way over to Monte's Hardware," he agreed. "I need some wax for my car." Roger's car is his pride and joy, so he's always washing, vacuuming, or waxing it.

Linda called Roger right before we were about to leave, so I didn't get to Patti's house until 5:15. When I went up to her room, I felt like I had stepped into a war zone. Stephanie was sitting on one side of the room with her arms crossed. Kate was playing with Patti's cat, Adelaide, on Patti's bed, and Patti was standing between them, frantically trying to figure out what to do. And no one was speaking!

Patti raced to the door. "It's just awful, Lauren!" she whispered. "They won't even *look* at each other!"

"I'll take care of it," I told her. "It's all my fault anyway." I stepped into the room and looked at Kate and Stephanie. "I don't want you two to be mad at each other on my account."

"Don't flatter yourself, Lauren," Stephanie said angrily. "I'm mad at you on Mr. Talbot's account!"

"I'm sure your Q.T. Pie doesn't need you to defend him," Kate jumped in sarcastically. "It's obvious that he means more to you than your best friends!''

"Me?" Stephanie screeched. "What about you?" Pretty soon, I was out of it completely, and Kate and Stephanie were at it again!

Patti puffed up her chest and bent backward. "Quiiiiiet!" she yelled. She's not usually that excitable, but things were getting desperate!

Kate and Stephanie looked up, totally surprised at Patti's outburst. "This is no way for best friends to behave," Patti scolded them. "And we definitely won't accomplish anything if all we do is argue. Let's just discuss this calmly — or we'll end up not speaking to each other until we're old ladies!" We couldn't help smiling at the thought of ourselves as angry little old ladies.

"Patti's right," Kate said apologetically. "I guess we got a little carried away."

"I just don't understand why you care, Kate," Stephanie told her. "You already did the dissection."

"But that doesn't mean I can't change my mind," Kate told her. Then she looked at me. "And it doesn't mean I can't stand behind Lauren."

"Kate's right," Patti agreed. "We don't have to agree about the dissection — just like we don't have to agree about other things. But Lauren might really need us, and it's important that the Sleepover Friends are there for her!" I smiled at her.

"Well, all right," Stephanie said. "I really didn't like being mad at you guys."

"Let's make a pact that no matter what each person decides about the dissection — or anything else — we'll always be best friends!" I suggested.

"Forever!" Kate, Patti, and Stephanie cheered. We all stood up and hugged each other.

"I, for one, am glad that's settled," Stephanie said. "I have a problem that I need your help with. My parents told me I couldn't get my ears pierced until I'm in high school. But I was thinking that maybe if all my friends got theirs pierced . . ."

"I don't know," Patti said hesitantly. "That's a pretty big deal. But I guess I could ask."

"Why not?" Kate said. "I never thought about getting my ears pierced before, but maybe it'd be fun."

I didn't want to be the only one to say no, now that we were all friends again. "It sounds like fun," I said. It was worth it to see Stephanie smile finally.

Roger had said he would pick me up at six o'clock so I could be home in time for dinner, but when I stepped into the Jenkins' front yard, I saw my dad's car sitting in the driveway — and both my parents were in the car! Usually only one of them comes to pick me up.

I said good-bye to the Sleepover Friends and slowly climbed into the car. "I thought Roger was going to get me," I said.

"We needed to talk with you about something," my father said. "Your new science teacher, Mr. Talbot, asked us to come in for a conference." Already? Before I'd even had a chance to talk to them? But they didn't really sound mad. In fact, I wasn't sure *how* they sounded.

"Mr. Talbot seems like a nice man," my mother added. Oh, no! They were going to take his side. I would have to do the dissection *and* probably be Q.T. Pie's least-favorite student of all time!

"He *is* nice," I agreed. "But what he's asking us to do is wrong. I just wouldn't be able to live with myself if I'd done that dissection."

My mother looked at me from the front seat. "We told him that if that's how you feel, we'd stand behind you," she said.

"So Q.T . . . I mean . . . Mr. Talbot isn't going to make me dissect a frog?" I asked.

My parents looked at each other. "He didn't

exactly say that," my mother said hesitantly. "But we told him we weren't going to make you. We'll write you a note tomorrow to give him."

It was great to have my best friends and my parents behind me, but how was I going to convince Mr. Talbot to agree with them?

Chapter
6

"Did Mr. Talbot call your dad for a conference yesterday?" I asked Hope as we walked down the hall to the science lab. Actually, it was more like *sleep*walking. Once again, I hadn't gotten much sleep the night before.

"Yeah, but my dad had appointments most of the afternoon, so they just talked on the phone a little while," she said.

"Well?" I asked, dying to know if Mr. Talbot had convinced Hope's father to make her do the dissection along with the rest of the class.

Hope looked confused. "Well, what?" she asked, wrinkling her forehead. "Oh! You mean what did my dad say?" I nodded. "He said he's opposed to dissecting animals, and he was glad I made the decision on my own."

I was relieved that I could count on her to be on my side. "My parents told him they'd listen to my side, and then make a decision," I told Hope. "When I explained how sickening the thought of dissecting an animal was for me, they wrote me this note." I pulled the folded piece of paper out of my back pocket. Hope smiled.

I had gigantic butterflies flying around in my stomach when I stepped through the science lab door. I went right to my seat without even looking at Mr. Talbot, and doodled in my "science only" notebook as he called roll. I didn't even look up when he called my name.

"Hope, you may go sit in the hall," Mr. Talbot told her when he finished taking attendance. She picked up her books and headed for the door. Wayne Miller started making gross noises with his mouth, but Hope didn't turn around. Wayne's a real creep, but Hope's too nice to tell anyone off — even a jerk like him.

Mr. Talbot ignored him, too, and went on with the class once Hope had closed the door behind her. "One lab partner from each set may get a worm out of the bucket." So the next victim would be a worm.

I raised my hand slowly while Mark Freedman stood up to go get our worm. Obviously, he knew there was no way I would do it. I had to wait a little while, but Mr. Talbot finally noticed my hand and called on me.

"May I please be excused, too?" I asked.

"Didn't your parents talk to you last night?" he asked.

"Yes, and they wrote me a note," I told him, not wanting to sound like a smart aleck. I got out of my chair and handed him the piece of paper.

David Degan pretended to be reading the note out loud. "Please excuse Lauren from science class," he said in a screechy voice. "She is a wimp and likes to cause trouble."

Mr. Talbot was too busy reading the real note to hear David. When he finished, he handed the note back to me and said firmly, "You may join Hope in the hall. And *no* talking."

Even though I knew what I was doing was right, I was really embarrassed to be the center of attention for the second day in a row. As I gathered up my things, Kate stood up. "Mr. Talbot, I'm not going to dissect a worm, either!" she announced, staring him straight in the eye. "I've thought about it since yesterday, and decided I don't think it's right!" Way to go, Kate!

Mr. Talbot didn't even try to convince her to stay, and I soon figured out why. He had another means of persuasion. "All right," he said. "Instead of sitting out in the hall, why don't you both take your books to Mrs. Wainwright's office? And tell Hope, too. That'll be better than the hall. Mark Freedman, please sit with Stephanie Green."

Mrs. Wainwright! That was the *last* person I wanted to see. Mr. Talbot obviously thought we were just trying to get out of class. He didn't believe that we honestly thought dissection was wrong!

As soon as Kate nodded her head, I knew it would be easier to face Mrs. Wainwright with friends — and better to face *her* than an innocent worm!

As we walked out the door, I noticed the most peculiar thing. Jenny Carlin didn't snicker once. And she wasn't flirting with Pete, either. Her eyes were sort of glazed over, and she was off in her own dream world. Something very strange was going on, and I was really curious to find out what it was.

Kate and I picked up Hope, and the three of us

walked to Mrs. Wainwright's office together. Mrs. Wainwright's secretary, Mrs. Jamison, smiled when she saw us. "Hello, girls," she said. She's super-nice.

Hope and I looked down at the ground uncomfortably, but strong-willed Kate spoke up right away. "Mr. Talbot sent us to see Mrs. Wainwright," she told Mrs. Jamison.

Mrs. Jamison announced us through the speaker on her desk and told us to go right into Mrs. Wainwright's office.

"Hello, girls," our principal said and smiled. "Where are Patti and Stephanie? It's not often I see the Sleepover Friends separated."

"Uh, they didn't come," Kate explained. "This is just our problem — kind of." Kate told Mrs. Wainwright everything that had been going on in science the past two days. She listened patiently and didn't speak until Kate finished.

"You girls do understand that the lab was built so you'd get a better science education," she said. "You can't learn very much sitting in the hall — or in my office, for that matter."

Hope finally spoke up. "It's not that we don't want to learn. I, for one, would rather be in the lab. I think it's a great idea," she told Mrs. Wainwright.

"It's just that Kate, Lauren, and I don't believe that dissection is the right way to be learning."

Mrs. Wainwright's eyebrows went up. "I can't say I agree," she said, shaking her head slightly. "But, I suppose if all your parents have excused you from class today, my hands are tied — at least for the time being. You may just stay here and read quietly until the period's over." She picked up her pen and started writing, and we opened our books.

But lunchtime was the worst. Just about everybody — even people I'd never even talked to before — were talking about Hope, Kate, and me, and what happened in science lab. For someone who doesn't like attention, I sure was getting plenty of it.

Ms. Gilberto had asked Stephanie to stay a little while after art class to talk, so Kate, Patti, and I went ahead to buy our lunches without her. We could hear all kinds of conversations about dissection — and ourselves — as we waited to get our enchiladas.

"Can you believe the way those fifth-graders are acting?" Carol Masters said as she ran her fingers through her long, straight blonde hair. Carol's in sixth grade, and she's so stuck-up, she usually wouldn't even talk about fifth-graders. "They were probably just trying to get Mr. Talbot's attention and fouled it up. Typical." She clucked her tongue against her teeth.

"As if he'd have any interest in *them* anyway," Carol's friend Julie Hines added.

As we walked through the line and back to our table, we heard a lot of similar comments. "People have been dissecting animals for hundreds of years," Walter Williams told a group of guys. "How can all those people be wrong?" Walt's only seven-and-a-half years old, but he's already in fourth grade because he's really smart.

A bunch of sixth-grade boys were huddled together talking. "What's wrong with those guys who are refusing to dissect a dumb old frog? I mean, what's the big deal?" I'd recognize that voice anywhere: Taylor Sprouse! Kate and Stephanie have both had crushes on him, but I think he's a jerk.

Ginger, Christy, and a couple of other girls from 5C were sitting together at another table. "I think they're making all the girls look bad," Ginger whined. "Now everybody's saying girls are wimps and can't handle stuff like this."

I decided not to defend myself unless someone was speaking directly to me, but all the nasty comments were really making me depressed.

66

The three of us sat down near Hope at our usual table. She'd already started munching on carrot sticks.

"I feel like I've committed a crime," I said as I set my tray down at the empty space next to hers and pulled out the chair.

"It's not so bad," Hope said, grinning. "A lot of people told me that even though they don't agree with what we're doing, they think that we should stand up for what we believe."

"And a few people told me privately that they agree with you guys," Patti added. "They're just afraid to say anything in front of their friends."

"Luckily, *we* have *great* friends!" Kate cheered. Patti smiled.

At that moment, the table shook like an earthquake had just hit it. Stephanie slid into her seat, breathless. "I couldn't wait to see you guys and find out how it went with Mrs. Wainwright!" she said and gasped for air. "I thought Ms. Gilberto would never stop talking. Are you guys all right? How did it go? What did she — "

"It's okay," Kate finally interrupted her. "She talked to us a little while and told us to read the rest of the time."

"But what's she going to do? Is she going to tell

67

Q.T. Pie to fail you?" Stephanie added. I'd completely forgotten about the grade since no one else had mentioned it. Suddenly I went from depression to sheer panic!

Kate and I shrugged. "She didn't mention it," I said.

"I think they have to give us an alternative assignment," Hope said. "That's what my dad said they did for him when he was in high school."

"Your dad's teachers excused him from a dissection lab?" Patti asked, sounding hopeful.

"Sure," Hope said, sipping her diet raspberry soda. "When he was at Riverhurst High." Hope's father grew up in Riverhurst before he moved to California. That's why her father decided to move back here after her parents got divorced.

"That means there's hope for us," I said excitedly.

"That was a long time ago. And that was in *high* school," Kate said in her "let's be practical" tone. "We're dealing with completely different people."

The more we spoke, the more nervous I could tell Stephanie was getting. Her eyes were as big as saucers as she listened to us discuss what might happen.

"Mr. Talbot said I couldn't get a good grade if

I didn't do the lab," I reminded the others.

"He just expects us to give in for the sake of our grades," Hope told me and Kate. "I doubt that he'll actually fail us. Besides, even if he does, our grades are good enough to pass for the year." That was easy for her to say. I usually get C's in science. If I failed one grading period, I'd have to work extra-hard the rest of the year to pass!

"Hope's right," Kate added. "Even though he's being a little unreasonable trying to make us do the dissection, he seems like a fair man."

"But you guys don't actually know what he'll do. He hasn't even been here a whole week yet. Maybe you *should* just give in," Stephanie suggested meekly. I began to wonder: How far would we go to stay out of doing a dissection?

Chapter
7

School on Friday went pretty much the way it had gone the day before. Everybody was talking among themselves about whether or not dissection was wrong — and whether we should be questioning our teachers. A lot of kids came up to me in the hall and the cafeteria to tell me what they thought. Even though I'd already made up my mind, I listened to everyone's point of view.

About ten minutes before the three o'clock bell, Mrs. Mead told our class to quiet down for an announcement. "Next week, there will be a special meeting of the PTA and school board," she told us. "Please be sure that you show this letter to your parents this weekend. This is not one of the regularly scheduled meetings."

"Maybe they've finally decided to give us six months off for summer vacation!" Henry joked as Mrs. Mead passed out the pieces of paper.

But the letter didn't say anything like that. I couldn't believe my eyes when I read the first sentence: *The topic of a special general meeting of the Riverhurst Elementary Parent-Teacher Association and the school board will be about whether or not children should be required to perform dissection labs.*

I was practically in a state of shock! Even though our names weren't mentioned in the letter, it was obvious that they were calling a special meeting because of Kate, Hope, and me! I had never imagined that not doing the dissection would create such a commotion.

I looked at Kate and then twisted around to look toward the back of the room at Hope. As usual, they both looked pretty calm as they read the letter. But I was too upset to finish it.

This wasn't about three kids and a few animals anymore! The school board only meets to make the most important decisions. What we were doing must be really important.

Of course, everyone else knew the note was about us, too. After the bell rang, a group of kids formed around my desk and Kate's. "Are you going to take it to the Supreme Court if the school board says you have to dissect?"

"Aren't you afraid that parents won't let their kids hang around you if you don't give in?"

"Why do you want to cause so much trouble for Mr. Talbot?"

I was so overwhelmed by all the attention, I couldn't even speak! I stood frozen by my desk.

Finally, Stephanie grabbed her book bag, broke through the crowd, and grabbed my hand. "Come on, Lauren!" she commanded. "Let's get out of here!" Patti was waiting for us by the door. We flew down the hall and hopped on our bikes.

The sleepover was in Stephanie's apartment that night. Roger and Linda dropped me off on their way to dinner. I thought I was the first one to arrive because I couldn't hear any regular sleepover noise outside the door. But after I knocked on the door and Stephanie let me in, I saw that I was actually the last one to get there, as usual. "Why is it so quiet in here?" I asked. "You guys aren't mad at each other again, are you?"

"No," Patti answered glumly. "It's nothing like that."

"We were just thinking about what's going to happen to you guys," Stephanie told me. "You know . . . with the school board and everything."

"We have to make sure *all* our parents go to the meeting — even the Jenkinses and the Greens," Kate told us.

"And maybe convince some of the kids who agree with you guys to have their parents go," Patti suggested. "They may be too scared to stand up to Mr. Talbot, but I bet their parents won't be."

"Aren't you afraid that if too many kids don't want to do the dissection, nobody will get to do it?" Kate asked Patti.

"Not really," Patti said. "Most of the kids want to do it. But the few who don't shouldn't *have* to. I think the school will just come up with a way to make everyone happy. After all, a big part of science is finding alternative solutions to problems — like using solar energy instead of coal!" I thought it was really great the way Patti always talked like a real scientist — *and* made so much sense at the same time.

Stephanie threw herself down on one of the red fold-out couches in the room. "I wish I'd never heard the word *dissection*," she said grumpily. "It's really messing things up big time!"

73

"Don't worry, Steph," I said, trying to console her. "By this time next week, the PTA will have made a decision."

Instead of consoling her, though, that comment threw Stephanie into a real panic! "What if they decide to send you to another school — one where they don't make kids do dissections!" she blurted out. "Because you live all the way over on Brio, they'll send you to Cooper Elementary, and Kate will probably have to go to Tall Oaks! The Sleepover Friends will be completely split up. Why can't you guys just give in?"

"I don't think they'd go *that* far," Patti said wisely.

Kate put an end to all our speculations. "There's no use worrying about it until they tell us what they're going to do," she lectured. "Sleepovers are *supposed* to be fun, but so far, this one is pretty boring!"

"Kate's right," Stephanie agreed. "I'm not being a very good hostess." She dumped a bag full of colored beads and stones, string, clasps, wires, and small tubes of glue on the floor. "This should liven things up, though! I bought us make-your-own-jewelry kits at Hale's Hobby and Craft Shop!"

"Wow, there's enough stuff here for us to make *tons* of jewelry!" I said excitedly.

74

"Cool!" Kate exclaimed. Even though she's not really into jewelry, I could tell that she thought it would be fun to make our own.

Stephanie showed us how to string the beads and twist the wires to make bracelets, necklaces, and earrings, and we all got started.

"I want to design some love beads," Stephanie said with a grin. "My parents brought some back for me a couple of years ago when they went to Haiti, but they broke last week."

"Who are you going to use your love beads on, Stephanie?" I teased. "Are his initials Q.T.?"

Kate rolled her eyes. "Who else?" she said.

Stephanie smiled.

"I don't think you'll need the love beads after all," I told Stephanie. "I made you something that's sure to attract Q.T. Pie's attention." I dangled a pair of earrings in front of her. I'd bent the wire in the shape of a frog and strung green beads on it. Plus, I'd added a small black pebble for an eyeball on each side.

"Thanks, Lauren," Stephanie said and laughed, taking the earrings. "These are great!" Then she frowned. "But these are for *pierced* ears. I can't wear these unless I get my ears pierced."

I felt kind of bad for reminding her. "Sorry,

Steph," I apologized. "I thought you could have them just in case your parents gave in about getting your ears pierced."

"Have you guys asked your parents yet?" she asked.

"You only asked us to talk to them a couple of days ago, Steph," Kate reminded her.

"I know, but this is really important. Please try to ask them before Monday," she pleaded. We all nodded. Then everyone was silent for a little while, thinking about how we were going to get permission to have our ears pierced, and working a little bit more on our jewelry.

Finally, Patti spoke up. "I made friendship bracelets for us so we'll never forget what great friends we are," she said as she handed us each a string of beads — in our favorite colors. Mine was blue, Kate's was yellow, and Stephanie's was red and black, of course.

"These are really beautiful," Kate said as she tied a knot in the ankle bracelet she was weaving and took the bracelet from Patti. Kate's ankle bracelet was all different colors with a shiny orange stone in the middle. "Thanks, Patti."

Suddenly my stomach growled like a grizzly bear! "I can't believe it!" I laughed. "We've been so busy talking about the school board meeting and making jewelry, we haven't gotten a thing to eat!"

"Call the newspapers," Patti giggled. "Lauren Hunter went an hour and a half without food!" Everyone cracked up.

Stephanie hopped up from the floor. "I could only fit the drinks in my refrigerator," she said. "I'll need help getting the food from the kitchen." The refrigerator in the corner of the apartment is just mini-sized.

"For peanut-butter-chocolate-chip cookies, I'll definitely help!" I said. Mrs. Green always makes up a batch of cookies when the sleepover's at Stephanie's. For a while, I had tried to be healthy and stopped eating all sweets. Even though I still try not to eat too many, I couldn't possibly go cold turkey on Mrs. Green's specialty.

We all piled out of the apartment, went across the yard, and into the Greens' kitchen. Stephanie's parents were there with her twin baby brother and sister. Mr. Green was trying to feed Jeremy, while Mrs. Green wiped Emma's orange face and hands with a wet cloth.

"Mashed squash night?" I asked, watching Emma turn her head to keep from eating anymore.

"Yes," Mr. Green laughed. "I can't say I blame

77

her for not wanting to eat it. It doesn't look very appetizing to me, either."

Mrs. Green made a face at her husband and turned to Stephanie. "I put the cookies in the refrigerator, honey," she said. "And you can help yourself to any of the leftovers from dinner, Lauren." I sort of have a reputation for raiding the refrigerator.

I found cartons of sweet-and-sour pork and fried rice and put them in a bowl. Patti grabbed four forks, and we carried everything back to the apartment. Patti and I poured the drinks, while Stephanie and Kate divided up the Chinese food.

"I got a movie for us to watch tonight," Stephanie said, smiling. She has a VCR in her apartment. *"September Again." September Again* is one of Kate's favorite movies. It was made in the 1960s, and the rest of us think it's pretty boring — especially Stephanie. I guess she was still trying to make up for their fight earlier in the week. I actually made it through the movie without falling asleep — even though Kate wouldn't let us talk while it was on.

After the movie, Patti pulled out her Mad Libs pad, and we played for about an hour before Stephanie decided she'd rather talk about Q.T. Pie — and, of course, Patti and Henry. Eventually, we all fell sound asleep!

Chapter 8

Monday morning, a few kids stopped to talk to me about dissection while the four of us were locking our bikes up in the bike rack. But they weren't just talking about whether it was right or wrong anymore.

Some people wanted help with the more practical issues — like how to get out of class. Usually, practical things are Kate's department, but she and Hope were keeping a kind of low profile about the whole thing. In fact, while I was talking to Lynn Peters and Vinny DeSilva, Kate, Patti, and Stephanie went on to Mrs. Mead's classroom.

"If you really want to get out of class," I told a group of kids from 5A, "you should have your parents write you a note. That's what I did."

By the time I had suggested it to the third group

that asked — a few sixth-grade girls — I noticed Jenny and Angela spying on me. It was kind of weird that they were just standing there, pretending not to be listening — even though I knew they were. But it was *really* weird that they never made any of their stupid remarks. In fact, they weren't even talking to each other. I knew they were up to something, and I didn't like being their victim one bit.

After Mr. Talbot took attendance, Sally Mason and Erin Wilson joined Kate, Hope, and me in Mrs. Wainwright's office during the dissection lab. By Tuesday, there were nine kids squeezed into the principal's office — including Jenny and Angela. Plus, some kids from other classes brought in notes from their parents to excuse them from doing the dissection, too.

Mrs. Wainwright finally stood up and peered at the protesters over her glasses.

"There's just not enough room in this office for all of you to get your work done," she said. At first she had been pretty calm about the whole thing, but I could tell she was starting to lose her cool! "Ms. Leonard is much better equipped to deal with you." Ms. Leonard is our librarian, and the library has a lot more desks and chairs than Mrs. Wainwright's office.

Mrs. Wainwright marched us down the hall. Ms. Leonard stood with her arms folded as we filed into the library. She and Mrs. Wainwright talked and nodded for a little while before Mrs. Wainwright slipped out the door.

Ms. Leonard cleared her throat the way she always does. "Mrs. Wainwright has asked me to monitor your study hall," she told us. "There is to be absolutely no talking, and you must read one of the books from the science section." She pointed to a section of shelves behind her. Breaking Ms. Leonard's no-talking rule usually means you have to do at least two book reports *and* stay after school one day to shelve books.

Donny McElroy and Charlie Garner let out a sigh of defeat. "Man, that's harsh," Charlie mumbled.

"Yeah," Donny agreed. "This isn't fun like I thought it would be." They dragged themselves over to the bookshelves and picked out a couple of books each.

As I watched Jenny and Angela go over to the bookshelves, it finally dawned on me! As icky as study hall sounded, Jenny was willing to do anything to get out of a regular class. And, of course, Angela followed her everywhere. A little while ago, Mrs. Mead wouldn't skip Jenny ahead into sixth grade, even though her test scores were pretty high, because Jenny didn't work hard enough on the assignments. As far as I can tell, she usually won't do any more work than the bare minimum to pass.

Not wanting to do the dissection must have been an act all along, I realized. At that moment, they were probably trying to figure out a way to get out of reading those science books, too. When Ms. Leonard wasn't paying attention, they would probably just pass notes.

Finally the day was over, and the four of us walked over to get our bikes.

"Isn't it amazing how so many kids are getting permission to skip the dissection?" I asked.

"I guess, but . . ." Patti hesitated. "Don't you think some of them might be doing it just to get out of class?" I couldn't believe how well she'd read my mind.

"I know," I said. "I can't believe the way Jenny and Angela are using the study hall just so they won't have to do science."

Kate breathed a heavy sigh. "I don't think that's — "

She didn't get to finish her sentence because a tall woman with short brown hair and green glasses

82

squeezed between us and pushed the others out of the way. She was holding a pad of paper in one hand, and a pencil in the other. "Are you Lauren Hunter?" the woman asked.

"Well . . . um . . . yes," I said. I was a little nervous. My parents had always told me not to talk to strangers, and this woman was definitely acting strange!

She put her pencil behind her ear and held out her right hand. "Pleased to meet you! I'm Lorraine Chambers — from the *Riverhurst Clarion*. I'd like to talk to you about the controversial things you're doing here at Riverhurst Elementary." The newspaper wanted to interview *me*? I couldn't believe it!

Kate, Stephanie, and Patti stood near the bike rack as I forgot all about my stage fright and tackled Ms. Chambers' questions. As we talked, a man with a camera crouched down and took my picture.

At first, the questions were pretty easy to answer. I had already talked to a lot of people about dissection.

Then she started asking tougher questions. "Do you intend to commit yourself to other causes?" I wasn't quite sure how to answer that. I thought about Hope and all the environmental causes she's involved in.

"Uh . . . yes," I searched for something to say. "The environment's important."

"Do you think recycling's essential for the survival of the planet?" Ms. Chambers asked.

Survival of the planet? How had we gone from frogs to life on the planet? But I couldn't back down now.

"Uh, yes," I struggled with the question. "In fact . . . I've . . . I've done my part to help that cause in this community. I've volunteered at the recycling center!" The Sleepover Friends had worked on a campaign to get local restaurants to recycle.

I didn't have time to think — her questions just kept coming. I tried to think of a good answer for each one. As the interview went on, it got easier to come up with answers. "The greenhouse effect? Yes, I think everyone should grow plants. . . . Acid rain? Sounds dangerous. It should be outlawed." Wow! I hadn't realized how much I knew about all these issues!

I felt proud once the interview was over. Ms. Chambers shook my hand and told me the story would appear in the morning edition of the paper.

"Gosh, I think people are really starting to take kids seriously," I said as Kate, Patti, Stephanie, and

I pedaled toward Hillcrest and Pine. "She was asking questions about a lot of important issues."

"Maybe that's true. . . . But did you really know what she was asking about?" Patti asked. "Some of those questions were pretty tough."

"Just because an issue's tough, we shouldn't ignore it," I reminded her. "A lot of kids never would have thought about the dissection if it hadn't been for me. Right, Kate?"

I turned around to look at Kate just as she was rolling her eyes at Stephanie. "Probably not, Lauren," Kate said, not realizing I'd caught her. "But I think you should give the others a little more credit. Stephanie was really the one behind the recycling effort. Some days she went down to the recycling center all by herself. You didn't even mention that!"

Kate was right. Even though I had helped out with the recycling campaign, Stephanie was the one who had gone around Riverhurst finding projects to get involved in. And she really had done most of the work.

"Sorry, Steph," I apologized.

Stephanie shrugged. "That's okay," she said. "That reporter was asking you a lot of hard questions. I'm sure it was difficult to answer everything."

I was glad she wasn't angry. I couldn't stand the thought of the Sleepover Friends arguing just as things were starting to get exciting!

"Hey, Lauren!" Willie Judd called as he pulled out of his driveway on his bike the next morning. "I saw your picture in the newspaper — pretty impressive!" Willie lives on Brio Drive, too.

"Thanks!" I smiled. I was running late that morning because I had had to wait until my parents finished reading the article before I got to. I knew there was no way I'd make it in time to meet Kate, Stephanie, and Patti at our corner, so I rode along with Willie.

"The article really made you look smart," Willie said and smiled. "I was wondering if I could talk to you about a few things?"

"Sure, Willie," I beamed. "I'd love to help out my fellow students." By the time we parked our bikes, I'd agreed to look into longer recesses, extended winter and spring breaks, and one cause I could really use: a later morning bell!

On the way to the science lab, a bunch of other kids mentioned the article, but none of the Sleepover Friends or Mr. Talbot said anything. I guess they hadn't seen it yet.

86

What Mr. Talbot *did* have to say wasn't exactly what I'd call good news! "I know that those of you who have been going to study hall during science lab have been working very hard," he said. "Since I'd hate for all that effort to go to waste, I'd like you each to write a three-page book report about one of the science books in the library." A written report? Yuck! What could be worse? "In addition, I'd like each of you to present an oral report on why you're against dissection — tomorrow." *That* could be worse!

A loud groan filled the room. "But one day's not enough time to write an oral report!" Erin Wilson protested.

"You've already thought about the issue. After all, that's why you're in study hall in the first place," Mr. Talbot said.

Giving an oral report is pretty bad, but it's not as icky as dissecting a frog. Plus, the report might be unpleasant, but the dissection was wrong! I had no choice. I had to do the report.

Unfortunately, most of the kids from study hall didn't agree with me. Kate and Hope followed me out of the room, of course, but everyone else stayed behind — except Jenny. She didn't even bring Angela with her! It was pretty easy to pretend to be reading a book, but how was she planning to fake an oral report?

"What do you think she's up to?" I whispered to Kate and Hope.

"Who . . . Jenny?" Kate asked. I nodded. "For once in her life, I don't think Jenny's up to anything — at least nothing bad."

I wasn't so sure, though.

Kate, Hope, and I sat at a table on one side of the library, and Jenny sat all alone on the other side. While the others started writing in their science notebooks, I was suffering from a major case of writer's block! Dissection was the only thing I'd been able to think or talk about for the past week and a half, and now I couldn't think of one thing to say! By the time we were dismissed, all I'd written on my piece of paper was my name.

Unfortunately, I couldn't talk about my problem with the Sleepover Friends at lunch. I'd promised a group of sixth-graders I'd help them organize a protest to get more school dances. Even though it wasn't really something that interested me, I knew they could use my expertise in leading important causes.

Chapter
9

We'd all planned to go to the mall after school that day since I needed to buy my grandmother a present. Her birthday was that Saturday, and my family was going to visit her in Bellvale. The four of us rode our bikes to my house so Roger could drive us to the mall in his car.

He was sitting on our front porch when we rode up the driveway. "It's about time, girls," he said, looking at his watch. "I was about to leave you behind."

"About to leave us? If we'd pedaled any faster, my legs would have fallen off," Stephanie complained.

I sat up front with Roger, and the others climbed

into the backseat. "We missed you at lunch today, Lauren," Patti said.

"Yeah, Henry was being really funny," Kate giggled. "He did a great imitation of Ms. Gilberto." The three of them laughed hysterically just thinking about it.

I was a little jealous I hadn't been there to hear Henry. "I wish I could have eaten with you guys. But right now a lot of other kids really need me to get them organized," I explained. "They sort of look up to me as a leader — even the sixth-graders." Since the newspaper article, just about *everybody* at school knew my name. It felt pretty neat to be a local celebrity.

"What kinds of issues are you tackling?" Patti asked.

"I think we should have three kinds of milk shakes in the cafeteria — instead of just one," I began. "And we need more sports equipment in the gym."

"Since your health kick started, you haven't even bought a milk shake," Kate reminded me. "And there's always enough equipment for everyone to use."

"Maybe you should concentrate on more important things," Patti added meekly.

"Like what?" I wondered, turning around to look at her.

Patti shifted a little in her seat. "Well, like things that mean as much to you as saving the frogs and worms in dissection lab. I guess we're a little afraid you might be losing perspective," she said.

I was starting to get pretty upset that everyone was ganging up on me. Stephanie could tell and came to my rescue. "Remember what we talked about last week, guys?" she asked Kate and Patti. "What's important to Lauren doesn't have to be important to you, too. And we promised to stick by her, no matter what."

Patti looked at Stephanie and then turned to face Kate. Kate shrugged and nodded. "Stephanie's right!" Patti finally said, smiling. "Let's just go to the mall and have a blast!"

Roger dropped us off at the entrance. "I'll meet you back here in exactly an hour and a half!" he called out as he pulled away from the curb.

"Let's stop by Perfect Scents," I suggested. "I think I'll find something for my grandmother there." We headed toward the store.

"It's been so hard getting us all together lately

that I keep forgetting to ask if anyone has gotten permission to get her ears pierced," Stephanie said excitedly.

"Sorry, Steph," Patti apologized. "I've been kind of afraid to mention it, but I don't think I'm really ready to get my ears pierced yet. I want to wait until I'm at least thirteen."

"And I've been so caught up in this dissection issue, I haven't really had time to talk to my parents about it," I told her. "Besides, I'm not sure how it would go over, and I don't want to bother them with anything else right now."

Stephanie hung her head as we walked toward the fountain in the middle of the mall. "Oh," she said, defeated. "I guess I'll just have to wait to get mine pierced, too, then."

Kate finally spoke up. "My parents gave me permission."

"What?" Stephanie, Patti, and I said in unison. Kate is the least fussy of all of us when it comes to appearance, and she was the last person who I imagined would get her ears pierced.

Kate looked at our stunned faces. "Yeah, my mom said she thinks I'm responsible enough to take care of them and everything," she told Stephanie. That's for sure. Kate is responsible with a capital *R*.

"I have to pay for it myself, but I've saved up enough already."

"I wish my parents thought I was responsible," Stephanie complained. "I mean . . . I did all those community projects, and I help Mom and Dad out with the twins all the time. I even take care of my own apartment."

I could tell Stephanie was a little jealous of Kate. She had wanted to get her ears pierced for quite a while, and it hadn't really mattered to Kate, but it was Kate who had gotten permission easily, and Stephanie who was having a rough time convincing her parents.

"You're right, Stephanie," I agreed, patting her on the back. "Your parents *should* give you permission. Maybe they will when they find out Kate's parents said it was okay for her. Now, I need your expertise picking out a perfume for my grandmother."

We squirted about twelve gallons of perfume on our arms. By the time I found the right scent for my grandmother, I wasn't sure I could really tell them apart anymore. But Patti, Kate, and Stephanie assured me that "Summer Spritz" was the best one.

After I paid the saleswoman for the perfume, there was still plenty of time left before we had to meet Roger. "Can we *please* stop by Be Jeweled?" Stephanie pleaded. Be Jeweled is the jewelry store in the mall, and we knew Stephanie wanted to look at the earrings. It's right across from Perfect Scents.

We never even made it inside the store, though. "Look at those earrings!" Stephanie exclaimed, pressing her nose against the window in front of the store. "They're the most gorgeous things I've *ever* seen!"

The rest of us looked at the pair Stephanie was talking about. They were dangles with a diamond in the center and little red stones all around it.

"Gosh, Steph," Patti gasped. "Those *are* pretty."

"Yeah, but they're not exactly in your budget," Kate said. "Did you see the price tag?"

"I guess they are a little expensive," Stephanie agreed with a gleam in her eye. "But they're so so-phisticated. And I'm sure they'd really impress Q.T. Pie."

"Even Ginger Kinkaid doesn't have anything that compares to those," I admitted.

Stephanie kept her eyes glued to the earrings. "I've just got to convince my parents to let me get my ears pierced!" she squealed.

"Don't you think you're concentrating too much on outdoing Ginger?" I asked Stephanie.

She finally turned away from the window with a confused look on her face. "What do you mean?" she asked.

"I'm afraid that you may be so worried about earrings and outdoing Ginger that you're forgetting about what's important," I explained.

Stephanie still didn't understand. "It's just that there are a lot of more crucial things to stand up for than getting your ears pierced — things that would benefit other people," I added. "Like some of the causes I'm getting into."

Stephanie was about to reply, but just then a couple of guys from 5A came over to talk to me and interrupted her.

"Hi, Lauren." Michael Pastore smiled. "Thanks for promising to talk to Mrs. Wainwright about getting an all-you-can-eat sundae bar put in the cafeteria."

"Yeah, with you speaking for us, how can we lose?" Kyle Hubbard spoke up.

"It's no problem," I said. "I'm glad I can help out."

"*You* volunteered to talk to Mrs. Wainwright?" Patti asked.

"Usually you'll do anything to avoid her," Stephanie reminded me — and everyone else.

I could feel my face turning red. Why did they have to say that in front of Michael and Kyle? They were looking up to me and counting on me to come through for them. I liked that feeling. But thanks to my *friends*, I now had to save face.

"*Usually* I will," I agreed. "But I sure have spent a lot of time in her office over the past week. Besides, I usually don't have anything this important to talk to her about. This is such a good cause, I'm sure I'll have no problem convincing her." I grinned at Michael and Kyle. I could tell they were impressed that I was willing to confront Mrs. Wainwright.

Just then Kathy Simons and Tracy Osner walked up. They're in 5A, too.

"Hi, you guys." I smiled. "How's it going?"

"It was going great until we found out about the reports we'd have to do for Mr. Talbot's class," Kathy said, frowning. I'd almost completely forgotten about the oral report that was due the next morning!

"Yeah, we decided to go back to the dissection," Tracy added. "At least we got to miss a couple of days of science."

"Besides, I kind of missed getting to see Mr.

Talbot! He's so cute!" Kathy added.

I was a little disappointed that they'd been so easily discouraged. But I couldn't expect everyone to be as committed as I was. Mr. Talbot's assignment *was* pretty hard. After all, even I was having trouble writing the oral report. But I was pretty proud of myself for sticking it out.

In the car ride home, I couldn't stop thinking about the oral report. I was kind of sorry that Tracy and Kathy had reminded me, because I was getting a sick feeling in my stomach thinking about it. I still hadn't been able to think of anything to say. I'd probably be up all night and still come up with zip!

"I guess you're probably having a lot of trouble writing the report for Mr. Talbot's class tomorrow, huh, Kate?" I asked.

"Not really," she said matter-of-factly. "I just have to recopy what I wrote in study hall today."

"Oh. Once I get home, I'll probably have no trouble writing it," I said, trying to sound confident.

"It'll be a cinch for you, Lauren," Patti reassured me. "After all, you're the leader of the antidissection movement!" I was too embarrassed to admit that their fearless leader wasn't really all that fearless.

The week before, I'd had no trouble telling Mr.

Talbot I wouldn't do the dissection, but now I was having a lot of trouble telling him *why*. Hope had helped me figure out that I thought dissection was wrong, but since our talk I hadn't really thought about why I believed that. And now I didn't have much time to figure it all out.

Chapter
10

By the time we all got back to my house, my parents had already left for the school board/PTA meeting. I was sort of glad that they weren't home. I didn't really feel like answering any questions about how things in Mr. Talbot's class were going. For the past week and a half, I'd had to update them at dinner every night.

Once Patti, Kate, and Stephanie got their bikes and left, I ate two pieces of the pizza my parents had left for Roger and me. Then I went up to my room to begin my report for the next morning. After an hour and a half, I was sitting in the middle of about a hundred crumpled pieces of paper — and I still didn't have any ideas!

I imagined myself standing in front of the entire class with a blank piece of paper in my hand. I tried to speak, but no words came out. Breaking the tense silence in the classroom was a shout from Wayne Miller: "I told you the wimp was just trying to get out of class!"

When I snapped out of my daydream, I started panicking. Mr. Talbot would think I faked the whole thing and never believe I feel dissection is wrong. He'd think it was no more important to me than it was to Jenny Carlin! I was so frustrated I put my head down on my desk — just as the phone rang. Saved by the bell!

"I'll get it!" I screamed loud enough for Roger to hear — even though he was probably stretched out on the couch and had no intention of moving one inch. "Hello?" I said, putting the receiver to my ear.

"Hi, Lauren," Patti's friendly voice said.

"Oh, hi, Patti," I said. "Boy, am I glad to hear from you. I'm having a lot of trouble figuring out what to say in my oral report," I complained.

"Maybe that's your problem," Patti said.

"What do you mean?" I asked.

"Maybe you're concentrating too hard on figuring out what to say. You're supposed to be writing about how you *feel*," she explained. I was really tired, frustrated, and confused, and Patti was only making matters worse!

"Don't you understand why practically everyone went back to doing dissections?" she asked.

"Because Mr. Talbot's assignment was too hard," I told her. Even as I said it, I realized that wasn't exactly the answer she was looking for.

Patti pushed harder. "But *why* was it too hard for them?" she asked. Then she answered her own question. "Because they didn't really believe it was wrong. They just wanted to get out of doing work. You thought it was wrong the whole time. You've just forgotten what was important to you."

Everything was becoming a little clearer. "So you think I'm having trouble writing the report because I've lost track of how I really feel," I said. "I've been so worried about what other people think of me, I've forgotten all about what I think of dissection."

"I don't think you forgot all about dissection," she said. "But because you were trying to lead too many causes, you may not have thought about it as much as you should have."

"I'm not even really *leading* the antidissection cause, though," I said mournfully. "Kate's already done her report, and I bet Hope's finished, too."

"That's because Hope and Kate are thinking about one thing — dissection. When dissection was the only cause you had to concentrate on, you knew how you felt. But when you started talking about all kinds of things that are important to *other* kids . . ."

"Okay, so I've been making promises to do things I don't really want to do," I admitted. "I don't like eating lunch with the sixth-graders. They're nice, but they're not the Sleepover Friends. And I was pretty scared about talking to Mrs. Wainwright for the fifth-graders. I don't even really think we should have a sundae bar! I guess I just liked being so popular."

"You've always been popular, Lauren. And even though they may not all agree with you, a lot of people respect you just for protesting the dissection lab," Patti said. "It took a lot of guts for you to stand up to Mr. Talbot and Mrs. Wainwright."

What Patti was saying made a lot of sense. I didn't need to make up causes to lead. I'd already led a successful cause. "You're right! I don't need a bunch of phony causes. Now I think I know what I want to say in science lab tomorrow. Thanks, Patti," I said.

"I'm not writing the report — you are!" Patti giggled through the receiver.

I was glad Patti had called. My writer's block had practically disappeared, and I was ready to get started on my report.

Just as I was putting the finishing touches on my paper, my mom and dad pulled up in the driveway. I raced down the stairs to meet them.

"How did it go?" I asked when they opened the door.

My mother looked surprised to see me. "What are you still doing up?" she asked. "You should have been in bed an hour ago!"

"I know, but I had to finish some homework," I told her. "Besides, I wanted to find out how the meeting went."

"It ran so late, the school board and PTA officers didn't have enough time to vote," my father told me. "They're going to have another meeting tomorrow so they can vote. We probably won't find out what they've decided until Friday."

"There were a lot of people behind you, honey." My mother smiled.

"Was Hope's dad there?" I wondered aloud.

"Was he ever!" My dad laughed. "He spoke for thirty minutes. And he really changed a lot of people's minds about animal rights — and kids' rights. He should be a politician!"

"I think he makes a better veterinarian!" I said and smiled.

My mom dropped me off on her way to work the next day. I wanted to get to school a little early to practice my report. Mark Freedman and Larry Jackson were already in 5B playing paper football when I got there.

"I can't believe the Sleep-in-Late Friends are here so early!" Mark sounded shocked.

"Actually, I'm the only one," I said. "The others are coming at the regular time."

"Lauren's probably here to lead an early-morning protest of the oral report," Larry said excitedly.

I shrugged. "No, it's nothing like that," I said. "I just felt like getting here early."

Larry and Mark looked a little disappointed that I was just a regular student who has to follow rules and do the work like everyone else. I guess they'd gotten used to my agreeing to protest everything. But the new Lauren was more sensible than that!

The new Lauren was more thoughtful, too. I felt like I owed Mark an apology for walking out on him in science lab. "I'm sorry I left you alone to do the dissection last week," I apologized. "It wasn't anything against you."

"That's okay." Mark grinned. "It was kind of fun working with Stephanie after Kate walked out, too. I never knew Stephanie was so good in science!" It could have just been my imagination, but I think Mark had developed a crush on Stephanie! I couldn't wait until our next sleepover to tell her — and Patti and Kate!

I sat down and silently read over my report. In practically no time, Kate, Patti, and Stephanie straggled in, and the late-morning bell rang.

"Boy, am I glad to see you!" Kate whispered as Mrs. Mead called roll.

Stephanie twisted around in her chair. "Yeah, we were afraid you wouldn't show up," she said.

"I just needed some time alone this morning. I think this report is going to be really great!" I said excitedly. We all made the thumbs-up sign.

After taking attendance, Mrs. Mead dismissed us for science. It was the first time in over a week that I would actually sit through the entire period. Even though I was pretty sure my report would go well, I was kind of nervous. After all, I wasn't exactly the teacher's pet! *I* knew I'd worked really hard on my report, but I wanted Mr. Talbot to know it, too.

Mr. Talbot called on Kate to give her report first. Of course, it was really well-organized. Mostly, she talked about how Hope and I had helped her to understand that dissection is wrong. "Even though friends can help you think through your feelings, they don't always have to agree with you," Kate said. Then she stopped and smiled at Stephanie and Patti. "And even though I now feel that dissection is wrong, I know that someday I may change my mind about it again."

Next it was Hope's turn. Her report was mostly about how all life on Earth is linked. She used the word *symbiosis.* Hope told us that's when two or more things benefit by living peacefully together. She also talked about how people shouldn't take living creatures out of their natural environment and destroy the balance of nature. The kids applauded both Kate and Hope, and Mr. Talbot looked pleased.

I had to go after Hope, which was tough since her report was so great! At first I was really nervous, but once I started to read I was less nervous. My report was different from Kate's and Hope's. I talked about why dissection is wrong, but I also needed to explain what I'd learned from my experiences over the past week.

"You should always stand up for what you believe in," I said, and looked Mr. Talbot right in the eye. "But it's also really important to remember what you're trying to accomplish. Doing what you believe is right shouldn't become a popularity contest. It's not important to get your name in the paper and have people ask you to be their leader. What's important is to know the difference between right and wrong. I learned that dissection is wrong, but I also learned a lot more."

After I finished, a lot of kids cheered and applauded, and Patti smiled ear-to-ear. She deserved a lot of credit for helping me write the report. Even Mr. Talbot looked impressed.

Then it was time for the last report. Jenny stood up and walked to the front of the classroom. I couldn't believe she was actually going to embarrass herself by giving a completely insincere speech.

Boy, was I surprised! Jenny talked about her poodle, Frisky, her Persian kitten, Fluffy, and how much her animals mean to her. Her speech showed that she'd put a lot of thought — and feeling — into the subject. "Frogs and worms and bugs have a reason to live, just like dogs and cats — and you and me," she said quietly. "We shouldn't think only of the way animals serve us. We also need to think about how they *feel*."

I realized that I hadn't learned everything about fighting for a cause until that moment. The entire week I had been questioning Jenny's commitment. But Jenny really did believe that dissection is wrong, just as much as I did. Even though she seemed to be thinking only about herself all the time, she obviously was a lot more thoughtful than I'd given her credit for.

By the time we'd all finished, there was just enough time for Mr. Talbot to remind us of our assignment for next Monday's class. "Everyone may line up and go back to 5B — except those of you who gave oral reports. I'd like to speak with you," he said firmly. Oh, no! Maybe I'd misinterpreted his reaction.

Stephanie and Patti waited outside the door for Hope, Kate, and me. They looked a little scared, too.

When I walked up to Mr. Talbot's desk with the others, he patted me on the back, and smiled at Kate, Hope, and Jenny. What a relief! "Congratulations, girls," he said. "I'm giving you all A's on the oral report part of your grade. You obviously put a lot of thought into this, and even though I still believe that dissection is an important tool for understanding animal and human anatomy, you helped me understand your views also."

Jenny didn't look smug the way she usually does. She just grinned a little and said, "Thank you." This was getting to be too much. If Jenny kept this up, I might actually believe she's human!

Unfortunately, not everyone was pleased to hear the news about the good grades. While Patti congratulated everyone, Stephanie made a face. "It's not fair!" she complained. "You guys act up, so you get A's and all kinds of attention. The rest of us slave over frogs and worms and we don't get anything."

"Don't you mean slave over jewelry-store windows and clothing stores?" Kate asked with a gleam in her eye.

Stephanie broke into laughter. "Well, maybe I have been trying to get Q.T. Pie to notice my great sense of style more than my scientific mind. But I've also been working really hard — especially at getting my parents to let me get my ears pierced!" The rest of us cracked up.

"Your parents still won't give in?" I asked.

"Not yet . . . but I think I'm softening them," Stephanie said. "I reminded them about all the extra

109

responsibility I've taken on since the twins were born. They looked like they were thinking it over."

Mr. Patterson's class passed us on their way to the science lab. Christy and Ginger are in that class, and as usual they looked great in their matching black jeans and polka-dot blouses. Plus, they were both wearing silver earrings in the shape of miniature palm trees. Of course they didn't pass up the opportunity to say something to us.

"Oh, look, Christy," Ginger said. "It's the Sleep-over Friends. Ugly clothes must have been on sale at the mall . . . and they bought everything!" She laughed at her own joke.

Patti, Kate, and I ignored them. We knew we could never compete with them when it came to fashion. Their parents take them shopping in the city and buy them whatever they want! But even though Stephanie looked fabulous in her red stretch pants and black-and-white-checked sweatshirt, she was really angry.

"Oh, those two make me so mad!" she fumed. "I'll show them who's got style." Then she looked a little worried and touched her earlobe. "My parents just *have* to let me get my ears pierced — soon!"

Chapter 11

I hopped right out of bed when my alarm went off Friday morning. That afternoon the entire school was going to find out the results of the school board/ PTA vote.

In a way, I was really excited about hearing the results. After all, this had become an important issue for me. But I was also scared. What if the school board decided that students had to do dissections? I'd have to do a makeup dissection lab. After everything I'd gone through over the past two weeks, there was no way I'd ever be able to dissect anything for the rest of my life!

Stephanie helped me take my mind off it for a little while. "Guess what!" she squealed as we walked to the assembly. Patti, Kate, and I shrugged.

"My parents said I could get my ears pierced — tonight! They're going to take us to the mall. Kate can get hers done, too!"

Kate squirmed. "Uh, I don't think I can," she said. "Don't you need to have your parents with you?"

"Nope. You just need to bring a note from your parents. My mom checked it out," Stephanie bubbled.

"I've never seen anyone get their ears pierced before," Patti said. "This'll be neat!"

Kate didn't look like she agreed with Patti. "I don't know about this, Steph," she said.

Stephanie started to get upset. "You promised, Kate! If you don't get your ears pierced, my parents will think I lied to them!" she pleaded.

"Oh, okay. If it means that much to you, I'll get my ears pierced, too," Kate finally gave in. Then she looked at me and Patti. "Are you guys sure you don't want to do it?" We shook our heads.

In the gym, we all sat on the edge of the bleacher seats waiting for Mrs. Wainwright to announce the results of the school board/PTA vote. By the time she finally stepped up to the microphone, I had only one or two fingernails left — I'd spent most of the morning chewing the rest of them off!

112

"The school board has decided that any student who chooses not to participate in dissection lab" — Mrs. Wainwright began. It seemed to take her an hour to get the rest of the sentence out — "will be given optional assignments on that topic that do not require actual dissection." Victory! She went on to talk about how she hoped that everyone would take advantage of the unique opportunity to learn science, but I didn't pay much attention after I found out I had won my battle.

After the announcement, the Sleepover Friends were so excited we grabbed each other and hopped up and down in a circle. Hope ran over and joined us. I looked at Jenny and gave her a weak smile. I knew that by Monday we would probably be just as nasty to each other as we'd been all year, but right now we were sort of on the same side.

David Degan came up behind us and said, "I finally figured out why you guys were so interested in saving a bunch of worms! They're your relatives!" He and Wayne Miller cracked up.

But most of the kids congratulated us. Even Walter Williams was pretty supportive. "I think you're making a big mistake by missing out on the dissection," he told us, "but it's great that you showed everyone kids can make a difference." Walter can be pretty creepy, but I thought that was a really nice thing to say.

That night we had a special sleepover celebration planned. After the Greens took us to the mall so Kate and Stephanie could get their ears pierced, we were going to stop by Charlie's Soda Fountain and pick up all the special fixings for a make-your-own-fountain-drink sleepover: chocolate and vanilla frozen yogurt — healthier than ice cream — seltzer water, milk, malted powder, and, of course, whipped cream! Then we'd make our masterpiece drinks at Patti's house.

"This is going to be so great!" Stephanie babbled as we walked through the mall. "I'm going to buy a new pair of earrings every week — maybe two! We can even trade earrings, Kate. I'm going to ask my parents to buy me a new pair for every birthday!" We walked into Be Jeweled. They do ear-piercing for free if you buy a pair of starter studs.

Mr. Reiner, the owner, came over to us. "Is there something I can help you with, young ladies?" he asked pleasantly.

"Yes, my friend Kate and I would like to get our ears pierced," Stephanie spoke up immediately.

Kate handed Mr. Reiner her note while Mrs. Green passed Emma to Mr. Green, who already had Jeremy under one arm. Emma and Jeremy started cooing in some secret baby language.

Mrs. Green signed a form for Stephanie and a form for Kate while Mr. Reiner went into the back room to get the ear-piercing equipment. Stephanie hopped up on a stool by the cabinet with earrings in it. He came back with a tool that looked like a gigantic hole-puncher.

Stephanie's eyes got round. "Uh . . . you go first, Kate!" she said as she hopped off the stool. Kate looked suspiciously at Stephanie and took her place.

"Isn't it interesting that even though we're a technologically advanced nation, we engage in such a barbaric form of self-decoration?" Patti said thoughtfully. We all turned and gave her strange looks. Patti shrunk back a little and shrugged. "It was just a thought."

By the time Patti had finished her thought, Kate's ears were done. One little gold stud sat right in the middle of each earlobe.

"Those look great, Kate!" Patti and I said in unison.

Stephanie scrunched her nose. "Did it hurt?"

"I didn't feel a thing," Kate told her.

"Go on, honey," Stephanie's mother encouraged her. "Your dad and I are right here."

"And the Sleepover Friends!" I added cheerfully.

"All right," Stephanie mumbled as she hopped onto the stool. Mr. Reiner marked each of Stephanie's ears with a pen as Stephanie sat completely still. In fact, she was so still, she looked like a zombie. When Mr. Reiner lifted up the ear-piercing tool, Stephanie sucked in all her breath, scrunched up her shoulders, and shut her eyes. The next thing we knew, she screamed and hopped off the stool!

"Stephanie!" we all yelled.

Stephanie turned beet-red. "I guess I wasn't as mature as I thought I was," she said weakly.

"But what about Q.T. Pie?" I asked.

"And Ginger and Christy?" Patti added.

"And *me*?" Kate screeched, pointing at her ears.

"Um . . . I think Mr. Talbot would be more interested in someone who works hard in science," Stephanie began. "And . . . uh . . . I can handle Ginger and Christy . . . and . . . well . . . I'm *really* sorry, Kate, but I just can't do it!"

"Well, I know one person you impressed in science lab, Stephanie — Mark Freedman!" I giggled.

Stephanie's eyebrows shot up. "Really?" Stephanie squeaked. I couldn't tell if she was happy or upset.

"I guess if we learned one thing this week, it's to stand up for what you believe is right. And Stephanie sure doesn't think getting her ears pierced is right for her!" Patti giggled.

I practically doubled over with laughter because of the look on Kate's face. She hadn't stopped glaring at Stephanie since she'd jumped off the stool. But she stopped being angry long enough to pay Mr. Reiner.

"You have to admit, Kate," I said as we headed back to the car, "it's pretty funny that out of all of us, you're the first to get her ears pierced!"

But Kate didn't have to admit anything. She crossed her arms in front of her and stared straight ahead.

Although I knew Stephanie felt guilty, I noticed she had a hard time keeping a straight face, too. And we knew that by the time we got to Patti's house for the sleepover festivities, Kate would have forgotten all about it. Even the twins seemed to know what was going on. They were gurgling and cooing in their baby seats.

It was great to have everything back to normal, and be with my best friends in the world on a Friday night! Everything was just perfect!

Sleepover Friends forever!

SLEEPOVER
FRIENDS

Super Beach Mystery

"If you're talking about the old house on the creek," the woman behind the counter said, "folks around here have been saying it's haunted."

"Haunted." Lauren nodded knowingly. She and Kate had just joined us.

"I think these people watch too much TV," Kate murmured.

I agreed with her. Okay, I was used to Lauren's runaway imagination. But adults talking about ghosts? Give me a break!

SLEEPOVER FRIENDS™

by Susan Saunders

Available wherever you buy books...or use this order form.

THE BABY-SITTERS CLUB

by Ann M. Martin

The seven girls at Stoneybrook Middle School get into all kinds
of adventures...with school, boys, and, of course, baby-sitting!

Collect
Them
All!

☐ NI43388-1	#1	Kristy's Great Idea	$2.95
☐ NI43513-2	#2	Claudia and the Phantom Phone Calls	$2.95
☐ NI43511-6	#3	The Truth About Stacey	$2.95
☐ NI42498-X	#30	Mary Anne and the Great Romance	$2.95
☐ NI42497-1	#31	Dawn's Wicked Stepsister	$2.95
☐ NI42496-3	#32	Kristy and the Secret of Susan	$2.95
☐ NI42495-5	#33	Claudia and the Great Search	$2.95
☐ NI42494-7	#34	Mary Anne and Too Many Boys	$2.95
☐ NI42508-0	#35	Stacey and the Mystery of Stoneybrook	$2.95
☐ NI43565-5	#36	Jessi's Baby-sitter	$2.95
☐ NI43566-3	#37	Dawn and the Older Boy	$2.95
☐ NI43567-1	#38	Kristy's Mystery Admirer	$2.95
☐ NI43568-X	#39	Poor Mallory!	$2.95
☐ NI44082-9	#40	Claudia and the Middle School Mystery	$2.95
☐ NI43570-1	#41	Mary Anne Versus Logan	$2.95
☐ NI44083-7	#42	Jessi and the Dance School Phantom	$2.95
☐ NI43571-X	#43	Stacey's Revenge	$2.95
☐ NI44240-6		Baby-sitters on Board! Super Special #1	$3.50
☐ NI44239-2		Baby-sitters' Summer Vacation Super Special #2	$3.50
☐ NI43973-1		Baby-sitters' Winter Vacation Super Special #3	$3.50
☐ NI42493-9		Baby-sitters' Island Adventure Super Special #4	$3.50
☐ NI43575-2		California Girls! Super Special #5	$3.50

For a complete listing of all the Baby-sitter Club titles write to:
Customer Service at the address below.

Available wherever you buy books...or use this order form.

Scholastic Inc., P.O. Box 7502, 2931 E. McCarty Street, Jefferson City, MO 65102

Please send me the books I have checked above. I am enclosing $ _____
(please add $2.00 to cover shipping and handling). Send check or money order — no cash or C.O.D.s please.

Name _____

Address _____

City_____ State/Zip_____

Please allow four to six weeks for delivery. Offer good in U.S.A. only. Sorry, mail orders are not available to
residents of Canada. Prices subject to change.

BSC790

APPLE PAPERBACKS

THE GYMNASTS™

by Elizabeth Levy